D1439099

MY LIFE AS A GIRL IN A MEN'S PRISON

Tiny Lies
When the Monster Dies
The Redstone Diary (co-editor)
Where Does Kissing End?
Borderlines (editor)
The Gambling Box (editor)
The Writer's Drawing Book (co-editor)
The Piano (co-writer with Jane Campion)
The Last Time I Saw Jane

MY LIFE AS A GIRL IN A MEN'S PRISON

Kate Pullinger

Phoenix House
LONDON

First published in Great Britain in 1997 by Phoenix House

The Orion Publishing Group Ltd
Orion House
5 Upper Saint Martin's Lane
London, WC2H 9EA

A catalogue reference is available from the British Library

ISBN 1 86159024 5

Typeset at The Spartan Press Ltd,
Lymington, Hants
Printed in Great Britain by
Butler & Tanner Ltd,
Frome and London

Versions of the following stories have appeared in anthologies:
'Celia and the Bicycle', *Storia 1*, Pandora, 1988
'The Dinosaurs of Love', *Storia 3*, Pandora, 1989
'A Modern Gothic Morality Tale', *Sex and the City*, Serpent's Tail, 1990
'A Kind of Desired Invasion', *So Very English*, Serpent's Tail, 1993
'My Life as a Girl in a Men's Prison', *Smoke Signals*, Serpent's Tail, 1993
'Dear All', *Bad Sex*, Serpent's Tail, 1993
'My Mother, My Father, and Me', *How Maxine Learned to Love Her Legs*, Aurora
Metro, 1995
'Forcibly Bewitched' and 'Charlie', *Forcibly Bewitched*, 1996

For Catherine Bryon

ACKNOWLEDGEMENTS

These stories were written over a number of years. Many thanks to Julian Rothenstein, Rachel Calder, Simon Mellor and Aamer Hussein; the Judith E Wilson Committee and Jesus College, Cambridge, where I was Visiting Fellow; and, once again, prisoners and staff at HMP Gartree.

CONTENTS

SMALL TOWN

I

PIGEON FANCY

There was pigeon shit everywhere.

He'd had to lean hard on the door and push with his shoulder. It gave with a slow crunch and he slid through the gap. Like stepping into a ghost room, a room that was a plaster cast of itself – only not plaster, but bird shit. Oddly white at first, then grey, black and yellow. An ordinary, square, furnished room. The door he came in and a door out the opposite side, a settee, a thin-legged table, a broken chair. Net curtains on the window, a sink below, exposed pipes where the cooker once stood. Everything coated in a layer of shit one inch, two inches, some places as much as six inches thick. How many pigeons? How many years? How could such a room exist?

★ ★ ★

He could see what she'd be like as an older woman. She'd have her own house full of odd books, the classics, anatomy, art, mostly second-hand, sheaves of music piled up around the boxed grand piano. She'd go to Greece on her holidays, drink retsina and look at the sea. She'd have serious relationships with men who'd think she was one thing, one way, until they learned that, in fact, she was not. She'd be metropolitan, wear gold-rimmed glasses on a gold chain.

And he would be old and conventional and he'd live in a small town and he wouldn't have seen her for years, but he'd love her, he'd still love her, even then he'd love her more than he'd ever loved anybody.

★ ★ ★

He arrived from Canada in the spring. It was part of the deal he had made with his dad – he finished his degree and worked for a year and was now having his summer of travel before heading home to start medical school. Peter was twenty-two. Twenty-two and still bargaining with his dad. He didn't know how he'd got so old – that was how he thought of it – got so old. But now he had escaped and, for a while, he was free.

London suited him. The Falklands War was on in the South Atlantic and the city steamed with fiercesome debate. He found a card pinned to a board in a radical bookshop – everything was strange in this city, even the notion of a radical bookshop was exotic to him – 'Come and Help Us Make a New City'. He took the tube under the Thames to Vauxhall. Across the wasteland next to the overhead railway line he could see a tenement building and he knew that was his destination. Peter had checked out of the youth hostel, he was carrying his backpack with him; once he arrived, he would be staying.

The building had five floors, centred round a large internal courtyard. He walked through an archway and into the bright space, dropped his pack and sat on the ground next to it. All around the noise of hammers and saws – through open doors he glimpsed people working.

After a few minutes, a young man wandered over. 'There's room,' he said, 'at the top.' He indicated a flight of stairs in one corner. 'With George.'

Peter picked up his bag and shouldered it. Everything was strange in London, this was only part of it. He went to look for George.

★ ★ ★

They took over two adjacent flats on the fifth floor. There were forty flats in the building, but the entire north side was uninhabitable, even for the DIY die-hards among the group. The roof had caved in and the rain had worn through, collapsing the floors and ceilings of the flats, storey after storey, right down to the ground. It reminded him of an old avalanche site in the Rocky Mountains near where he was born. In the early part of the century a ramshackle, hard-hewn mining town called Frank had been obliterated when half a mountain slid down onto it in the night. One person – a baby – survived, a little girl Peter had always imagined was thereafter known as Frankie. No one had seen the slide take place, there was no one to see, they were all asleep. These days the highway ran right through it, across it, the road lined with enormous ragged boulders. A small plaque on one of the rocks told the story; Peter and his family would stop their car to read it from time to time. Now, in London, Peter wondered if anyone had witnessed the slow-motion avalanche at Vauxhall Palace Buildings. Probably not, he thought, the place had been empty for years.

On the fifth floor the flats were one-bedroom: landing and sitting room at the front, bedroom and kitchen following on in the middle, narrow bathroom and, facing into the courtyard, toilet outside on a small balcony. Everyone had their toilet outside on the balcony. In the morning the courtyard echoed with flushing. George decided right away that this wasn't enough room for them both; Peter stood and watched as he fetched up a sledgehammer and proceeded to knock a hole through the sitting room wall. 'On the other side,' he explained between bashes, 'will be another sitting room, same as ours. We'll only have to do the kitchen and bathroom on this side, but we'll have all this extra space.' Peter went back into the kitchen, to escape the dust. In the week he'd lived in Vauxhall Palace he'd been taught, after a fashion, how to weld pipes, how to run wiring. He lay back down on the floor and continued attempting to plumb the sink.

By the end of the day George had knocked a hole the shape of Frankenstein's monster through the wall. He called to Peter, who climbed through after him. The sitting room next door was identical to the one they already occupied, empty except for a large, pale, deco-style bureau that stood beneath the front windows. 'Cool,' said George, running his finger through the dust. Peter walked down the hallway towards the bedroom, which was furnished, the plain double bed neatly made as though expecting its tenant that night. At the window he pushed back the curtains, orange and blackened with age, and saw that the rear end of the flat was avalanche afflicted, collapsing into the ruin of the flats next door. It looked as though the kitchen was probably still intact, and he went to have a look. That was when he put his shoulder to the door and discovered the pigeon sanctuary. George, in his effete Australian way, was disgusted by the sight and the smell, although to Peter the room simply smelt old. When he was younger his father used to tell him he had an underdeveloped sense of smell, he was odour-blind, like some boys were colour-blind. But Peter knew his sense of smell was fine, he just happened to like tangs and aromas, a good whiff and you knew where you stood. A quick guide to intimacy. Now when his roommate shouted and rushed away from the room, Peter thought he heard a stirring — wings. From the corridor George called out, 'You can have this side, Peter, you're Canadian, you're used to wildlife.'

So Peter was happy in his London flat, his bijou squatted London property. In the evenings he and George cooked together, weird and economical combinations of rice and beans, they'd both become sudden vegetarians. Afterwards they'd venture down the street to the off-licence to buy beer, which they'd carry to the ground floor flat that had been converted into a meeting place, a speakeasy. A sound system had been rigged up and the walls painted black where they weren't knocked through to create more and larger spaces. Some nights people showed slides or films; everyone living in Vauxhall Palace seemed to be an artist, or at least, at art school, Goldsmith's, Camberwell, St Martin's, Chelsea. They all did things with their hands. There was a lot of talk about world politics, about the work on the flats, the best way of finding furniture, bathtubs, cookers and sinks, about the possibilities of a money-free economy. Peter didn't say a lot, but he listened. Amanda, Simon, Katherine and Will, and then the ones with nicknames, Squeak, Ziggy, Baby. And Fancy, the girl called Fancy, Peter wasn't sure whether that was her real name or not.

★ ★ ★

He slept between the sheets that someone had drawn up and corner-tucked years and years ago. The first night they smelt a bit musty and felt a little damp, but the double bed was luxurious compared to the youth hostel, compared to the floor of the sitting room on the other side of Frankenstein. Peter wasn't used to hardship, even though he'd been a student for four years; he was soft in his North Americanness, central heating, dishwashers, microwaves, cars. He'd lain awake for a while, mulling over the plumbing he'd done, wondering if he'd got it right. They'd find out soon enough, when they turned on the mains tomorrow. He could hear music filtering up from the speakeasy. He'd left at three a.m., and people were still drifting around, talking, dancing, George in a corner with Amanda, both giggling wildly. The music died suddenly, and Peter was held close by the night.

He woke at first light with the sound of pigeons. It took a few moments to understand what he heard – at first he thought perhaps George had been successful with Amanda – were they having sex outside his door? It was a human sound, but then its humanity fell away – cooing. That breast-full bird sound, early morning. He got up and went out into the corridor. When he opened the door to the old kitchen he was met with sudden movement, the air filled with mad fluttering. He stepped forward, the crust under his bare feet like a rough beach of drying seaweed. The birds fled through a hole in the ceiling before he could see them. He went back to bed and dreamed of flying.

Once the kitchen and bathroom were plumbed in and functional, they got on with decorating. Peter had never been one to look at walls and consider colour schemes, but

6

George went at this task with passion. 'It's got to look good,' he said. 'It's got to be somewhere I would like to be.' George was in a band, although Peter had never met the other members, never heard a strain of their music; he planned to turn his bedroom into a recording studio and spent his days arranging the wiring. Everything was legitimate in Vauxhall Palace, at least in their flat, the electricity and gas metered up, the appropriate boards notified, and they had every intention of paying their bills. They might have looked and talked like subversives, but Peter knew their souls – his soul – had a thick layer of small town underneath. Peter's veneer of anarchy was very thin, thinner even than George's, three weeks thin, the length of time he had been in the UK.

★ ★ ★

Fancy's flat was on the second floor of Vauxhall Palace, on the opposite side of the courtyard. Peter knew this because as he was coming out of the toilet on the balcony one day, he saw her going into hers. She was wearing a long T-shirt, and her legs were bare, as were her feet. He was relieved when she didn't look up – he didn't like the idea of her knowing he'd just been to the toilet. But he didn't mind knowing what Fancy was up to – it made her seem more normal, more real. He had spoken to her several times at the speakeasy. Once they had a conversation about Canada. She didn't know anything about Canada, except that it was part of the Commonwealth which had something to do with the Queen. She'd certainly never heard of Alberta, and she told him that her best friend in infant school had had that name. Peter wondered what infant school was – a school for tiny babies? – but he didn't ask. He thought that if he asked for explanations every time he didn't understand something in England he would become known as the Question Mark King.

Fancy had been to art school as well, she'd only recently graduated – textiles. She was a weaver. She told Peter she also did silk-screening and print-making on fabric and he noticed her thin fingers were always stained with ink. 'They don't have art schools where I come from,' he said.

She looked at him blankly. 'I wonder what happened to my friend Alberta? We lost contact.'

Peter found English people difficult to comprehend, but he liked them, with their quiet, convoluted ways, so unlike the folks back home. He got on well with George, but George was Australian and also new and confused. Peter made friends with another of their neighbours, Joseph, who was a Catholic from Belfast – Peter knew this was politically significant but didn't quite understand how or why. Joseph declared an immediate sympathy with people 'from across the water' and he told Peter they'd be mates because they both pronounced their 'r's' properly. 'Those English,' he said, 'they let their r's evade them. Smokah,' he waved his cigarette, a roll-up, in the air, 'filtah – it won't do. A sure sign of moral laxity,' and he laughed and laughed until Peter laughed as well, uncertain of what was making them so happy.

Peter got a job, which he hadn't intended. This was meant to be his summer of freedom and fun, but he found having to think of something to do every day rather taxing and thought a job would help him structure his time. And it would be easier on his savings. He worked in a take-away patisserie, a vaguely unpleasant shopfront

8

across the Strand from Charing Cross Station. He spent his four-hour shifts down in the airless basement filling croissants from a giant vat of béchamel that a frightened Argentinian – 'Colombia, I come from Colombia,' he insisted – cooked up. Peter knew Roberto was Argentinian because when asked that's what he said every time, before growing flustered and correcting himself too emphatically. Peter did not press the point and only mentioned the Falklands once when he asked Roberto what he thought of the war.

'Nothing,' said Roberto, 'I think nothing. I come from Colombia.'

The basement was hot, made hotter by the ovens, and they worked shirtless, their backs sliding wet. When Peter cycled home across the river after work he felt the breeze dry his underwear.

At night he and George would go to the speakeasy. Eventually George and Amanda got together and the early morning sounds of the pigeons became mingled with the sound of the lovers who seemed to feel free to make love all over the conjoined apartments, with the exceptions of Peter's bedroom and the ghost kitchen next door. At these times Peter felt lonely, and he was rather glad of the company of the birds. In the morning he would stand at his bedroom window and watch them arrive and depart from the eaves. He would draw himself up and think of the girlfriends he had had at university and tell himself he could do it again, there was no reason to think the only women who liked him were those in Alberta – and thinking of Alberta made him think of Fancy and her infant friend and he lay back down on his hundred-year-old sheets. He liked to think of them as hundred-year-old but, in fact, they were made of nylon –

pink – and he knew they probably came into being during the synthetic 1970s, the last time Vauxhall Palace was inhabited.

He determined to try harder with Fancy. That night at the speakeasy he spotted her friend Katherine. 'Where's Fancy?' he asked politely.

'Off somewhere with Tony, I should think.'

'Tony?'

Katherine looked at Peter sideways, as though his interest in Fancy piqued her interest in him. 'Oh Tony, don't you know Tony? He's been in love with Fancy since she was four.'

Peter felt himself pale.

'That's what they say. Tony was mates with Fancy's older brother and when he dandled her on his knee she gurgled and that was it for him.'

'Do they go out?'

'They're practically married. But if you ask me –' Katherine leaned forward, 'Fancy's bored with him. He's so old! Nearly thirty.' She clapped her hands and laughed.

Peter shared his beer with her. Joseph stopped by for a chat, cadged a cigarette off Katherine, then wandered away. Katherine told Peter about her current project – she was painting a replica of Michelangelo's Sistine chapel on the ceiling of her bedroom. 'Those fingers,' she said, 'they're very difficult.'

Just when Peter was beginning to wonder if he should concentrate on being nice to this girl instead of the other, Fancy came along and sat on Katherine's knee. 'Hello,' she said, leaning to one side, her arms around her friend's neck. 'Hello there,' and she winked at Peter. She hauled herself upright and nuzzled Katherine's cheek.

'Leave it out,' Katherine said, neatly sliding out and

away from Fancy's grasp. 'I'm going to find Simon.'

'Hi ya,' said Peter, nodding his head, feeling as though he was coming over all cowboy.

'Hello,' said Fancy, carefully placing an elbow on the table to steady herself. She was a little drunk. 'I'd like to get to know you. Alberta.' She giggled.

Peter pushed his last can of beer towards her. He got up and moved around to her side of the table. Fancy shifted nearer and they put their heads together. 'Britain has no rightful place in the South Seas,' she declared. 'Give back the Malvinas.' Her breath smelt of apples.

'I've got a friend who's Argentinian.' Peter thought of Roberto working in the heat of the kitchen.

'You do? she said, moving a little closer. 'I would like to meet him.'

'I'll try to arrange it.'

They talked about the speakeasy – who was there that night, who was not – Peter's job, Fancy's work. They talked about the present, immediate things. She wore a sleeveless vest that hung off her thin shoulders, he glimpsed a white cotton bra underneath. No one interrupted them and the hour got later and the black walls moved closer, the music grew softer although it still carried with it a harsh edge – the Test Department, the Velvet Underground, Crass, Lee Perry. Fancy kept her hand on Peter's thigh.

After a while he was desperate to take a piss. When he was drunk he found he couldn't bring himself to use the word 'loo', it seemed too silly, undignified. Back home they said 'john' or 'can' but those words were no good any more either. He got up and told her to wait right there and almost wished he could tie her to the seat so she wouldn't move away.

The toilet was outside in the courtyard and to get there he had to pass through a series of small rooms. He entered one that had been painted red since the last time he was through – the night before? – walls, floor, ceiling. People sat on decrepit stuffed chairs and sofas, Amanda and George in one corner. Peter stood in front of them and started to talk, but they looked at him as though he was speaking from the bottom of the sea. 'Peace man,' George said. He held up his hand, fingers in a Star Trek V. Amanda said 'Shh,' then closed her eyes and fell asleep.

He got back to their table and Fancy was gone. Peter sat down in despair. The room was full of cigarette and druggy smoke, and for a moment he longed to take a bath. A voice behind him began to sing. A song about going out to Alberta, where the weather's good in the fall.

It was Fancy and he stood up and danced a slow dance with her as she sang. He had hated that song as long as he could remember. But she knew all the words, and she led him out of the speakeasy, across the courtyard, upstairs to her flat.

★ ★ ★

Nearly a week passed before Peter bothered to look inside the bureau in the sitting room on his side of Frankenstein. He and George used the other sitting room for lounging, drinking instant coffee, reading newspapers, this one relegated to thoroughfare. A footpath led from the hole in the wall through the dust down the corridor to his bedroom. In the middle of the floor, like a snow angel, was the imprint of a human body – Peter guessed George and Amanda had made love there the night before. He strayed off the path, stepped onto the ghost bodies, and opened up the double front doors of the heavy yellowing piece of furniture. Inside sat a white china teapot with its own round and shiny chrome teacosy, and two white china cups and saucers. He took them out carefully. Both side cupboards and the drawers were empty. He carried the china through to the kitchen. After work he'd invite Fancy for tea.

George was lying in the bath. 'Make me a cup of coffee, will you, mate?' he called out.

'I'm leaving for work.'

'Oh,' said George. 'Dag,' he added half-heartedly.

It was unusual for Peter to see George without Amanda now. Since they'd got involved George had become less animated, quieter, as though the two of them added together somehow made less than one person. Peter didn't mind, although sometimes he felt as though his friend was disappearing. And he was a little envious. Fancy was proving elusive. There one minute, vanished the next, like something he had conjured.

George was not a tidy roommate. Peter didn't mind, he washed the dishes and cleared the table but didn't bother with much else. George had hung a black curtain in the bright bathroom and when he was on his own, he was often in the bath soaking. Peter had never been a big bather himself, at home he had always taken showers, but showers didn't seem to be part of the landscape of the British bathroom. So when he came home after a morning at work, streaked with cream sauce and smelling of baked cheese, he learned to bathe, even though it felt to him like something one did last thing at night.

And this morning he had managed to find Fancy at home; he invited her to come round later for tea in the new teacups. He clattered up the stairs with his bicycle over his shoulder, trying not to bounce it against the wall on every landing. Inside the flat there was a peculiar smell. He leaned his bike against the wall and walked through the kitchen. George had boiled the kettle dry, there was water across the floor where he'd got out of the bath and flung the kettle from the cooker into the sink. The wall next to the cooker was blackened. Peter felt suddenly dismayed by the untidiness and, thinking he would mop the floor and clean the kitchen in preparation for Fancy, went into the bathroom to get the mop. They did possess a mop, George had found one in a skip.

The room was dark and fuggy and Peter drew back the curtain. When he turned, he almost lost his footing, there was so much water on the floor. George was still in the bath. His head rested on the rim and one arm dangled over the side and Peter thought he looked like David's painting of Marat just after he was murdered by Charlotte Corday. Strapped around his arm was a piece of rubber tubing. An empty syringe lay on the puddled floor just out of his reach.

Peter stepped forward, unsure of his footing, unsure of how to view this scene. It was beyond him, and he knew it, he felt his Albertan childhood all around and it did not include lying in the bath all morning, syringes, black curtains, speakeasies. He took another step. The water in the bath was cold. But George was warm, in fact when Peter moved closer he heard the faint sound of George snoring. Once Peter knew he was not dead, he realized his roommate looked happy, content, comfortable even. So Peter took the mop and went back into the kitchen. He concentrated on getting ready for Fancy.

They had slept together, just once, that night when

Fancy sang 'Four Strong Winds' as they danced. They'd gone into the sitting room of her flat and she turned on the radio. 'My stereo got nicked,' she said. 'I've got loads of cassettes –' she pointed to the shelves – 'but nothing to play them on.'

'I've got a stereo at home,' Peter said, and hated himself for mentioning 'home', for even thinking of Alberta when his new home was here, for bringing up his previous life. But Fancy didn't notice. She sat on the cushions piled next to the wall. He sat down beside her.

'Would you like a cup of tea?' she asked, but he moved close to her, drawn in by her smell of apples.

In the morning Peter woke with sun on his face. He sat up and a piece of paper fell to the floor. 'Good morning! Gone to market,' it read. His arm had pins and needles. In front of him, taking up most of the room, was an enormous loom, a thick and complex piece of woven and patterned fabric emerging from it. It was as though the loom had materialized with the morning, he had not noticed it the night before. He got up and walked around it and was reminded of a piece of farm machinery, it was somehow pre- and post-industrial simultaneously.

★ ★ ★

He finished cleaning up the kitchen in preparation for her visit and was wondering what to do about the burnt kettle when there was a knock at the door. On the way up the corridor he considered what he was wearing – he was filthy, his newest white T-shirt smudged and sticking. He suddenly realized it didn't matter, this was what everyone in Vauxhall Palace dressed like. He felt happy; Fancy was coming to tea.

He opened the front door and there she was, and

behind her a tall guy Peter didn't recognize. He tried to stop himself from frowning.

'This is Tony, Tony, this is Peter,' Fancy said as she moved past. Peter stepped aside and let Tony pass as well. Tony who, according to Katherine, had been in love with Fancy since she was four.

'Glad to meet you,' Peter said, 'come on in,' but they were already in the kitchen, seated at the table. 'Would you like a cup of tea?'

Fancy nodded. 'Tony wanted to see your flat, didn't you Tony? It's always interesting to see what other people are doing to their places.'

'You live here Tony?' Peter had thought he knew everyone in the flats.

Tony nodded. 'No milk in my tea.'

Fancy was standing, moving around the kitchen, inspecting.

'Would you like a piece of cake?' On the way home from work Peter had bought a Jamaican bun loaf; they could eat it with butter. There were only two white china teacups – he tried not to worry.

Tony shook his head. He turned to Fancy and said, 'We will be late.'

'I know,' said Fancy.

Peter was boiling water in a saucepan. In Alberta, he thought, I would probably ask them to explain. Late for what? What are you doing? Who is this guy? Let's be frank. He remained silent, afraid to turn around in case he found them kissing.

'When can we meet your Argentinian?' Fancy asked.

'Roberto? I guess I could bring him to the speakeasy one night,' Peter said, uneasily. 'Yeah, he might like that.' Roberto would love the speakeasy but he would be unhappy to discover that Peter did not believe he was Colombian and had, in fact, been telling the world he was Argentinian. 'I'll ask him next week.'

He poured the tea and cut the cake. No one spoke.

After a while Fancy said, 'Where's George?' and Peter said, 'How's Katherine?' and the door to the bathroom swung open and George stood there in his towel, looking refreshed, smiling sleepily. 'Hello Tony,' he said, 'got anything on ya?'

Tony shook his head.

'I'll be off then,' said George, 'people to see.'

★ ★ ★

After that, Peter felt a little low for several days. He didn't know what to say to George about the syringe, and he didn't know what to say to Fancy. He felt he had found her and lost her already. He went to work and, afterwards, hung around with Roberto. Roberto was obsessed with the British Museum; he was viewing the collection room by room. Peter accompanied him to Ming Dynasty Chinese Porcelain. They progressed from display case to display case very slowly. Roberto didn't speak, he looked from item to item, reading all the text carefully. 'What is "pigment"?' he asked Peter in the middle of the room. Peter explained as best he could, and when he felt he couldn't look at another vase, he began to examine the tourists. All the women had characteristics – an ear, a hand, a smile – that reminded him of Fancy.

He couldn't bring himself to mention the speakeasy to Roberto, and on Friday night he went along on his own. He drank a couple of beers and talked to people he suddenly felt he had grown to know rather well – Joseph, Simon, Katherine, Squeak. Around midnight Fancy

17

emerged from the red room at the back. When she saw him, she came straight over. 'I don't know what those people see in that stuff,' she said sharply.

'What stuff?'

'You know. Smack.'

Peter took a breath. 'What people?'

'What people? Tony. George. Amanda. Amanda, for God's sake. I've known her for ages. It's like a secret club.'

Peter nodded.

'Let's go,' she said.

They emerged from the speakeasy into the night, wandering away from the tenement onto the wasteland. The large empty space was ringed with streetlamps, but it was thick black and unlit in the centre. They headed into the dark. The night air was unusually warm, like summer nights back in Alberta. 'If you close your eyes,' he said, 'and block your ears, and plug your nose, we could believe we were out on the prairie.'

'It reminds me of Leamington Spa,' she said.

Fancy turned and put her hands on his chest. He realized he was at least a foot taller than her. She pushed against him and they fell backwards slowly onto the hard ground. She lay on top of him and made small movements adjusting their clothing. A freight train went by on the overhead tracks. The breeze blew dust into Peter's eyes, but as he raised his hand to wipe it away, she began to kiss him. She kissed him hard, with much more force than she had the night they spent together underneath her loom. She bore down on him and soon he found himself inside her. She rocked back and forth and he clutched her breasts and she moaned and later he would see with great clarity that this was the moment they conceived her pregnancy.

18

2

GIRL ON A MOTORBIKE

In the summer between high school and university, Peter travelled north to work on his uncle's ranch. He left the south-west corner of the province where his own family lived in the foothills of the Rockies and drove north-east to between Red Deer and Edmonton where the land stretches out flat. That spring his father had loaned him money to buy a motorcycle. His mother had objected, but only half-heartedly, as if it was something she thought she should do but didn't really feel. The motorcycle was a surprise, it had never occurred to Peter to want a bike, he didn't think of himself as that kind of guy. When he daydreamed about forms of transport it was always aeroplanes he saw himself boarding, jumbo jets with vast, expansive wings. But of course, once he had the money and was standing in the local garage with its rich smells of oil and overalls, he fell in love with the machine before him, black, low and gleaming.

He drove it to school the next day and impressed the hell out of everyone, including his teachers — no one there had seen the Motorcycle Boy in him before either. And one month later he hit the highway on it, heading up to his Uncle William's cattle ranch. He had a room in the big house and didn't do anything as prosaic as help out with the horses and livestock, his uncle employed skilled and seasoned men for that kind of work, real cowboys. The ranch was very prosperous, mostly because of the oil rig that stood in a far-flung corner. Although his uncle owned the rig and took all the profits he liked to pretend it didn't exist and that he was still an old-fashioned down-home rancher. Peter was assigned the tasks his uncle couldn't find time for, cleaning machinery, painting the outbuildings, helping his Aunt Lisa cook for the men. The O'Briens hadn't been able to have children of their own and while they did not treat Peter like their own son, they were fond of him in his role as odd-jobbing employee. The pay was good and, with his motorcycle, he had a certain amount of freedom on the long summer days, so hot he sometimes thought he could hear the skinny trees around the house crackling as though they might burst into flame.

Late afternoons he would drive the twenty miles to the nearest town and the general store where they sold cold drinks. One day while he sat on his bike drinking his coke and eating potato chips, the local youth arrived en masse in a souped-up pick-up truck with an elevated axle, flames painted down either side of the body, a clapped-out Honda hatchback, and a motorcycle. Four boys got out of the truck, four girls out of the car, and a fifth person stretched off the bike. He watched as the biker lifted off the helmet, feeling mildly superior because he didn't wear one, and saw that it was a girl. She looked his way.

'Hi,' she said, smiling. Her hair was curly and dirty blonde, her eyes brown, and when she smiled her nose crinkled. Her friends had already gone into the store. 'Nice bike. You're not from around here?'

'I'm working for the summer out at my uncle's, William O'Brien.'

'Oh, O'Brien's, yeah. What's your name?'

'Peter.'

'Helen.'

They both smiled and Peter could think of nothing

further to say. He brought the coke bottle to his lips, and gave the rim a wipe when he saw that it was coated in dust raised by the vehicles.

'Maybe I'll come out and visit you – ' she indicated her bike.

'Is that yours?'

'I saved up my baby-sitting money for four years,' she said, laughing.

'My dad loaned me the money for mine.' He wished he hadn't said that, it made him sound spoiled and rich. Her eyes widened.

'Boy,' she said, 'lucky.' He thought maybe she was being ironic.

As they spoke the others were beginning to reappear outside the store. Helen made a movement as though to draw him near and introduce him to her gang, but he held back. He wanted to talk to her, not all of them. 'Well,' he said, starting up his bike, 'come out to the ranch and see me. Any time.'

'All right,' she said, smiling, 'I will.'

Peter peeled off onto the highway. It was easy to be cool on a motorbike.

A couple of days later Helen did show up at the ranch. After dinner, around seven, Peter was helping his Aunt Lisa with the clearing up. Every evening she cooked a big meal for all the ranchhands and her husband; every morning, and every lunch time as well. Peter was doing the washing up, he was wearing an apron and rubber gloves and listening to rock music on the radio. His aunt went to the door. When he turned around Helen was standing in the kitchen, watching him. 'Hi ya,' she said. He waved at her with his pink rubber hand. She sat at the kitchen table while he finished the dishes.

'And Bob and Karen are getting married in September, and that's about it for around here. I tell you, it's boring. I get so bored I could scream. What's it like where you live?'

He removed the gloves, snapping each finger off one at a time. 'The town is a little bigger, but not much. Small enough to know everyone.'

'That's the worst thing, isn't it? Knowing absolutely everyone. Never seeing anyone or anything different.'

'People come and go a bit.'

'They do? Well, count yourself lucky. No one's come or gone here for years.' She laughed and he smiled as he noticed once again how her nose crinkled.

They went outside and sat on the porch. It was still light, and very warm. His aunt had disappeared deep into the house, and his uncle was back out working with the men. Helen had parked her bike right next to his. He thought they looked happy together.

'Hey,' she said, 'let's go for a ride.'

'Okay,' he said, 'good idea.' He followed her off the porch. She had left her helmet behind this time.

They took the rutted road out to the highway, heading east away from the town. The wind felt good, and the sky was turning pink and orange with the sunset, so he didn't mind too much that they couldn't talk. Helen pulled ahead, and a few miles down the road he noticed she was signalling to the left. He turned off the highway and stopped next to her.

'Longest and straightest and flattest stretch of packed dirt road in Alberta,' she said, indicating the way ahead. 'Goes way out, past Carter's ranch, a hundred miles at least.' She smiled at him as if she had a plan that she expected him to have guessed. 'You ready?'

'Sure,' he said, revving his bike and taking off ahead of her. He watched the needle on his speedometer rise, and was surprised when he heard and then saw Helen come up alongside, overtake him and speed on ahead. She was lying flat, her body stretched along the seat of the bike, hands gripping the bars and the accelerator, legs trailing behind like those of a bird in flight, her hair plastered back against her head. Above the noise of the bikes he was sure he could hear her whooping and shouting.

She began to drop her speed. He came to a standstill beside her as she sat up swiftly and balanced the bike. 'See?' she said. 'You get the bike going and lie down at the same time. Then you go as fast as you can. You've got to try it, it's the best, it's the best feeling.'

He watched as she took off again. He started his bike and lifted his feet from the pedals, lowering himself down onto the warm gas tank, flipping his legs out behind. He felt an odd sensation in his gut, like vertigo, like he'd stepped off the cliff for real this time, except he was unafraid. It wasn't difficult to balance, the bike was moving fast, and soon he caught up with her and they were travelling side by side lying hard against their thrumming machines and it was the longest and straightest and flattest stretch of dirt road in Alberta, and they were going faster and faster and it was more like flying than flying could ever be.

After a while he heard her lose speed, so he took his hand off the accelerator. He dropped behind and watched as she swung her legs and raised herself upright. He felt flattened by the tremendous momentum and couldn't manage to get himself upright, so when he pulled over he fell off his bike into the dirt. Helen was off her machine and laughing at him, and running out into the field of wheat. He pushed the bike away, got up and shook off the dust, like a wet dog shakes off water, and followed after her. The grain was so dry that it cut and chafed against his arms and legs as he ran. Up ahead she tripped and disappeared among the sheaves and when he came upon her he threw himself down next to her, laughing and winded, his spirit still accelerating. And Helen kissed him, and he kissed her back, and they lay there together, touching and kissing. Their pulses slowed and he felt he was swooning.

Helen sat up. 'Let's do it,' she said, 'let's just do it. I don't care that I hardly know you.' She pulled off her T-shirt and undid her bra, sudden white against her brown skin. They spread their clothes out on the ground, both keeping on their underwear, and the sky was so red it was black. They held each other close, and kissed with their eyes shut, and he wondered if she felt as shy as he did. With the sweat and the dust and the grain she smelt wonderful and eventually they took off their underwear and he was inside her and it felt even better than stretching out on the speeding motorcycle.

Later, they sat up and she rested between his legs. The night was so bright and clear he could see the little hairs on the back of her neck, soft golden hairs that made him think of goslings.

When he got back to the house his aunt was watching television and his uncle had already gone to bed. 'I'm sorry, Aunt Lisa,' he said, 'were you waiting up for me?'

She smiled benevolently. 'Did you go out with Helen Gordon?'

He nodded.

'She always seems a nice girl. I knew her mother, back in the days when Will and I used to go to church. But then we found we had better things to do than religion.' She paused. 'Where did you go?'

'For a ride on our bikes.'

'A girl with a motorcycle,' Aunt Lisa said. 'I wish I'd had a bike when I was her age. I would have driven straight down that highway away from here, I can tell you that much.'

Peter was a little shocked. 'I didn't know you wanted to get away.'

'Everybody wants to get away when they are your age,' she said, turning back to the TV.

Peter and Helen took to driving out together several evenings each week, the nights when Helen wasn't busy making her fortune baby-sitting. Sometimes they would go down to the river, and make love on the wide, slow bend. Other times they would return to their stretch of dirt road; in their passion they flattened a considerable patch of Carter's wheatfield, scattering imprints of their bodies throughout the grain. They talked a lot, about their families mostly. Peter thought it was as though Helen was biding her time, waiting for something to happen, not him, but something bigger. She had no real plans, and was unimpressed by and uninterested in Peter's future at university. On Friday nights they met up with Helen's friends from high school, the crowd of couples from the flaming pick-up and the clapped-out Honda Peter had seen that first day at the general store. They drank beer down at the river, and Peter grew to know and enjoy their jokes and their stories. After a month he felt as though he had been there with them forever.

The summer grew hotter, the mosquitoes and black-flies intensified, and the smell of their sweat and sex became mingled with insect repellent. Helen had what she thought was a brilliant idea; she bought boxes of mosquito coils and when they went out into the fields at night she would make a circle of them at twelve-inch intervals along the ground where they lay. The smouldering coils stank and stung their eyes, and Peter worried that they might set the entire field alight, but it did keep the bugs away and he could run his hand along her smooth skin and not find her back smeared with blood and wings.

At the ranch Peter had embarked on cleaning and repairing the hayloft in the big barn furthest from the house. It was a gruesome job, the unmoving air so thick with dust he thought his lungs might simply give up and stop functioning, some afternoons he couldn't even manage to cough. The loft was alive with enormous spiders and tiny mice and he banged his head on the sloping roof and shouted with fright so many times it became part of his routine. When she had time his aunt would come up to help him, bringing a jug of apple juice and ice. They'd sit on the edge of the loft and look down into the barn and she would tell him about what she might have done had she had a motorcycle and driven away down that highway.

'I've always wanted to go to London,' she said as Peter gulped his drink. 'Not because of the Queen or any of that guff, but just to see the streets. I'd like to walk around Piccadilly Circus. Piccadilly Circus!' she laughed. 'It isn't a circus, you know, with animals and things. What on earth do you think it could be?'

'Why don't you and Uncle William go? You could get away in the winter, couldn't you?'

'I know, I know, and it's not as though we can't afford

it –' Lisa often made sly references to the fact that she and William had money, money that they seemed unable to spend. 'But your uncle says he doesn't like to travel – not that he's been anywhere. We went to Vancouver on our honeymoon twenty years ago.' She began to laugh again. 'Big deal!'

'Maybe you should go without him.'

Lisa turned slowly and looked at him. 'You are a bright boy,' she said, and changed the subject.

Peter's uncle and aunt took it as given that Helen Gordon had become his girlfriend. Every so often they invited her to dinner, but after the first time when Peter saw Helen at the table surrounded by the big ranchhands all of whom she seemed to know by name, he decided they were better off on their own with a picnic. One night, at the end of July – Peter had been on the ranch for nearly two months by then – they went down to the river to eat. Helen had been in a strange mood when they met at their appointed place out on the highway; he tried to kiss her and she moved away. Now she was sitting on the opposite side of the blanket, as far away from him as she could manage.

Peter offered her some potato salad on a plate.

'I don't want anything,' she said. 'I feel sick.'

'You do?'

'Yeah. I feel like puking. In fact I am going to puke.' And, indeed, Peter watched as Helen got up, walked behind a tree, fell onto her hands and knees, and threw up. He went over to her, reached out to touch her back, but she sheered away from him as though he'd been about to smack her. Later she returned to the blanket, curling up under one corner as if she was cold. She didn't speak, so Peter thought it best to leave her in peace. He put the food away and lay back on the blanket and looked up at the stars. They were too many, too bright, to count, but he had lived all his life under such skies. After a while, it occurred to him what was wrong with Helen. He too began to feel cold.

'Are you sure?' he asked.

'Yes, I'm always regular, every twenty-eight days, like it says in the books. It's been forty-six days now.'

'Forty-six!'

'It's a lot, isn't it?'

'Forty-six.' He moved over nearer to her, placed his hand on her back. She was very hot. Peter felt calm. 'I didn't even think about birth control.'

'Aren't we a pair then.' She smiled a little. 'Somehow I thought that, you know, doing it outside, that you couldn't get pregnant if you did it outside.'

'You mean if you weren't in a bed?'

'Yeah.' They laughed and then fell silent. 'Fat lot of good those endless sex education classes at school did us,' she said eventually.

Peter tugged at Helen's shoulder, rolling her over into his lap. Her breath was sour as he bent to kiss her face. He undid the buttons on her shirt, pulling the cups of her bra down. He moved his hands over her breasts. It was true they felt changed, and he had noticed, but put it down to the odd and lovely strangeness of the female body. He ran his hand down her stomach and into her jeans, slipping it warmly between her legs. Helen bit his other hand and they made love differently that night, Helen on her hands and knees, crying out, Peter behind her, clamped on, straining. It was as though they were older, darker, more fierce.

They didn't make any plans, there didn't seem to be

anything to plan, it had happened, it was happening. Peter lived with it in his thoughts and out of his thoughts at the same time. Helen remained calm. She didn't pull away from him again, now that he knew. Sometimes in the evenings if she was baby-sitting he joined her. On the couch in front of the television he tried to imagine what it would be like if this house was their house, if the kids upstairs were their kids, if this was their life. He didn't think about it too hard when he found that he couldn't, that his imagination wouldn't travel that far. They didn't talk about it, except every once in a while Helen would look up at him and state a figure. Fifty-one. Fifty-four. Sixty. One day he took it upon himself to ask how many days there would be in total. She didn't reply, and her look was mean.

And then four days passed and Helen didn't come out to the ranch to visit, didn't call. Peter began to worry, all the vague questions that had been mumbling away in his head suddenly articulated. Should he drop out of university and marry her; can you drop out when you haven't even started? Could he pay for her to go somewhere, where? Montreal? Toronto? or could you have it done in Calgary? What would his parents say? What about Aunt Lisa? When he went round that evening to where she usually baby-sat, Kathy, one of the friends from the gang, was there in her place.

'Where's Helen?' Peter asked when Kathy came to the screen door.

She spoke through the mesh without opening the door, as though she knew something about him she didn't like. 'At home. She's sick.'

'Really?' Peter asked, his stomach tightening. 'What's wrong?'

'I don't know,' said Kathy, 'you'll have to ask her yourself.'

Peter drove across town to Helen's house. As he travelled down main street he was tempted to squeeze the accelerator and lie flat on the seat and see what the town looked like from that birdy, speedy angle, see how fast he could leave it behind. But he turned sedately up her drive instead.

Mrs Gordon came to the door. 'Hello Peter,' she said, 'Helen thought you might be round.' Her expression was placid and welcoming.

'Is she okay?' He spoke a little too quickly. He didn't want to appear nervous.

'She's been feeling a little green around the gills.'

Peter went up the carpeted stairs and knocked on Helen's bedroom door.

'Come in.'

She was lying on the unmade bed in a pair of men's pyjamas. An upright fan blew a breeze lengthways along her body and the room was strewn with bits of paper, as though the fan had been allowed to redistribute the contents of the desk and wastebin. He paused at the door, and then went forward and sat on the bottom end of the bed. She winced.

'Are you all right?'

Helen's face was blank. 'Yes.'

Peter fought to control himself, all the questions in his head. The fan whirred past him every few seconds.

After a while Helen spoke. 'My mum doesn't know. She didn't guess.'

'I haven't told anybody.'

'Good.'

Peter didn't feel he could ask if she had told her friends.

He thought about Kathy behind the screen door. There was a long silence.

'Have you ever seen the Frank Slide?'

'The what?'

'The big avalanche, at Frank, near the BC border.'

She didn't reply.

'We should go there sometime. It's . . . amazing.' He fell silent again.

'I want you to do something for me,' she said.

'Okay. Anything. I'll do anything.'

'That's not necessary. Just do this one thing.' She indicated her desk. 'The brown paper bag.'

Peter got up, pulled the chair away from the desk, and retrieved the bag which was stuffed full of what felt like cloth, he couldn't see in the dark room.

'I want you to get rid of them. I don't care how. Burn them. Whatever.'

Peter nodded. 'Okay,' he said. 'Anything else?'

'No. That's all. That's it, Peter. That's all. Goodbye.' She turned over and rolled towards the wall. The breeze from the fan lifted her pyjama shirt. He saw the mild furrow that her spine created along her back. Although he wasn't close enough to see it, he knew that her skin was lightly covered with soft gold hair, so fine as to almost not exist. He hated that her farewell sounded so final. He wanted to lie with her on the bed. He clutched the paper bag to his chest instead, and turned and left.

He got on his motorbike, wedging the bag between his legs. Suddenly feeling very tired, he drove out to his aunt and uncle's ranch. He put the paper bag on the chair next to his bed where he could see it, and went to sleep.

He woke at first light, picked up the bag and, without considering where he should go, found himself on his bike heading down to the wide bend in the river where he and Helen had so often been together. He left his shoes on the seat, but didn't bother to roll up his jeans. Where the river water meets the smooth mud he turned the bag upside-down and emptied it. The contents fell out in a clump. He sorted through the items one by one, pulling them apart. Two sheets, one fitted. Two bath towels. Rigid and stuck to themselves with – after a moment he realized – blood. And gristle. Peter stood stock still as he understood what he was looking at. He stepped back hard into the water as though the gang was there and someone had given him a playful shove. Losing his balance, he fell forward and grabbed for a handhold, pulling a sheet with him.

As it hit the water the sheet sank, and then rose up again, billowing. Peter hung onto a corner as the river attempted to pull the cloth away. He felt the sheet strain like an animal trying to escape from his grasp. He watched as the bright blood began to rinse out – to him this seemed miraculous. After a few moments the floral pattern re-emerged. He let go, and the sheet floated away. He scrambled up onto the bank and kicked the other sheet and the towels into the water, scraping his foot hard against the root of a tree. They too sank and then slowly rose, like great underwater birds taking flight, floral sheet and towels pastel pink, coming clean in the sun, the green and silver glinting river water washing them away.

3

GOTHIC

Peter went into work one day to find Roberto had gone.

'Deported!' shouted his boss. 'Would you credit it? Turns out he wasn't Colombian at all, but an Argie!'

'Oh,' said Peter, heading down to the basement before the man could say another thing.

The job was harder to bear without Roberto to share it, without Roberto and his tales of Great British Museums and their marvellous contents. Now it just seemed hot, and the pay-cheques too small, and the new cook's béchamel tasted disgusting. There wasn't any reason to stay, Peter was adding savings to his savings which was contrary to what you were supposed to do during your summer away. So he quit.

By this time George's smack habit had become full-blown, gothic. He and Amanda had grown pale and thin; they both wore black, Amanda with strategic splashes of purple that only served to show up the damaged veins in her neck and hands. When they were high they were impossible to talk to, and when they were normal they were obsessed with sorting out their next hit. Peter had read somewhere that it was feasible to be a junkie and function completely normally, to treat the habit like a small, secret and much loved pet you kept hidden in your room, but it wasn't like that with George and Amanda. They'd turned into large and swirling smackheads locked in a lurid drama of their own making, a kind of morbid sitcom that Peter found very boring. He was angry with George, and felt he'd lost yet another friend.

He and Fancy continued to spend time together; she

told Peter she was well and truly rid of Tony. He spent afternoons pottering around her flat while she sat at her loom. He was working his way through her shelf of books. Sometimes they listened to the radio, which always seemed to be tuned to the farming programme 'The Archers'. Peter couldn't follow it even though Fancy was happy to explain the plot to him endlessly. One weekend she took him home to meet her parents in Leamington Spa. It went all right, although they were made to sleep in separate beds and Peter was surprised that Fancy accepted this without arguing. He offended her parents when he referred to their garden, their lovely big garden with its hedges and roses, pergola and pond, as their 'back yard'. 'Back yard,' Fancy's father had guffawed, 'is that what you call it in the colonies?'

Fancy knew that she was pregnant after her period was only a couple of days late. She stood in front of her loom with her legs planted firmly to the floor and her arms crossed tight across her chest. 'I'm pregnant,' she announced, her expression unreadable.

Peter didn't know how to respond. It's the second time, he thought, I've made the same mistake twice. I'm only twenty-two and I've fucked it up twice. He'd assumed she was on the pill. He moved towards her and Fancy let him take her in his arms.

'I'll arrange for a termination,' she said. 'We can get it on the NHS. Hopefully I won't have to wait too long.'

A termination, he thought, I've never heard it called that before. Final sounding, and yet, euphemistic, vague. Time for your termination, darling. All trains terminate here. He felt relieved for a moment and then was overwhelmed with guilt that she would have to bear it, not he.

'I had one last year,' she said, her face hardening. 'I know all about it.'

Peter held her tight in bed that night, although he avoided touching her belly. He thought she smelt different, somehow fresher and older at the same time. She fell asleep right away but later on woke him with her crying.

'What's wrong?' he whispered.

'It will hurt,' she said. 'It did last time.'

He shivered and sweated, and rocked her to sleep.

He accompanied her to the clinic for her pregnancy test, the subsequent meetings with doctors and counsellors. He was always the only man in the waiting room and the other women looked at him suspiciously. He tried to appear solicitous, good-natured, reliable, sweet, feeling as though it fell on him to redeem his reputation, the reputation of all men responsible for unwanted pregnancies. Fancy was very calm, even when they were told she would have to wait four weeks until the hospital could book her a place. She didn't exhibit any outward signs of being pregnant, and Peter watched her carefully. She stopped eating, saying she didn't feel like it any more, and after a while her ribs began to protrude a little. She wanted to keep living as though nothing had changed, nothing was altered in any way. She kept on working at her loom, listening to the radio, making and drinking endless cups of tea.

One day Peter walked into his bedroom and found George and Amanda asleep in his bed, on his pink nylon sheets, sharing his pillow, like twin Goldilocks in a bad dream. He shouted at them, and shooed them away, as though they were pigeons visiting from the next room.

They gathered their things and looked at him mournfully. 'Sorry mate,' said George. 'We got a bit lost.'

'Just get out,' Peter replied, although he knew what they meant, he felt that way himself these days.

After that, George and Amanda stopped using the flat as their base. Peter assumed they were spending their time slumped in a corner round at Amanda's. When it became clear that they weren't coming back, he embarked on a cleaning campaign. He got rid of the piles of newspapers and empties, he washed the dishes, the floors, the windows, cleaned the fridge, the cooker, the bathroom. He borrowed a vacuum cleaner from Fancy and went so far as to Hoover the curtains, their makeshift ones as well as the ones left behind by the flat's previous occupiers. Now he was no longer working he became increasingly houseproud. He invited Fancy round to his place in the evenings, cooked for her and tried, unsuccessfully, to make her eat.

Fancy wouldn't spend the night with him at his flat. She couldn't stand the sound of the pigeons. She hated hearing the quiet movements and soft flutters emerging from the ghost kitchen as the birds settled in for the night. 'I just can't get used to it,' she said. 'I don't see how you stand it.'

'It's not a case of getting used to it,' he tried to explain. 'I just like it, that's all. They reassure me.'

One morning he went into the toilet on the small balcony and discovered a couple of twigs on the floor. He got the broom and swept them away before heading out to do some grocery shopping. He came back, put everything away in the cupboards, went into the toilet again and found another pile of twigs, neatly arranged in a circle. He thought the wind was playing tricks and swept them away. He went over to Fancy's for the rest of the day.

They stayed up watching a movie on TV. He held her close to him on the settee, felt her deep and calm breathing. In the commercial break, she spoke quietly.

'I wonder if I ever will have a baby,' she said.

He took a breath. 'Sure you will. If you want to. When you're ready. Some day. You're only twenty-one.'

'We could go out to Alberta,' she said, 'weather's good there in the fall.'

He smiled and watched the movie.

'Do you want children?' she asked a bit later.

He had never thought about it. 'I don't know,' he said. 'At the moment getting pregnant seems like the worst thing that can happen.' He felt her stiffen. The movie came back on. 'Well, maybe not the worst thing,' he said.

When he got back to his flat late the next morning, he threw open the window and ran a bath in his clean bathroom that smelt of fresh cleanser and bleach. He got undressed and, wearing only a towel, went out onto the balcony. On the floor of the toilet was a nest. Inside the nest was an egg. A small, translucent grey pigeon egg. Peter looked at it, appalled. He went back into the kitchen and fetched a plastic bag and the dust brush. The nest was a pathetic affair, bare and thin and straggly, as if the pigeon had not realized on each of its return visits that its previous efforts had been swept away. The egg itself rested on bare concrete. Peter brushed it up and refused to think about whether or not he had broken the shell. He tied the ends of the bag together, put it in the rubbish and carried it out and down to the courtyard before getting into the bath.

That night he and Fancy went to the speakeasy. They hadn't been for a while, their news had made them anti-social, had made them want to hide away. Beforehand they walked to the off-licence and between them bought a large bottle of rum and another of coke. Then they went and sat in the room with the loudest music and proceeded to drink the night away.

Around two a.m., George appeared at their table. 'You going home?' he asked, his voice roughened, as though he'd been in a fight.

'Maybe later. We've still got this to drink.' Peter indicated the bottle. He and Fancy had been dancing and he was having a good time.

'No, I mean . . . what I mean is: are you going back to Canada?'

Fancy had never asked Peter this question. He looked at her now, she was watching him closely. 'Hello George,' she said, but neither she nor George took their eyes off Peter. He seemed to need an answer with some urgency.

'I don't know,' Peter said. 'I guess so.' He looked at Fancy again. 'I don't know. Why is it so important all of a sudden?'

'I'm going back to Oz.'

'You are?'

'Yeah.'

'But why? You seem to be . . . having a good time.' Peter thought of George lying like a corpse in the bath.

'That's the point, isn't it,' he said, suddenly adamant. 'That's just it. Got to go home, don't I, back to Mum and Dad. Away from this place.' He passed his hand slowly through his hair.

'What about Amanda?'

George shrugged. 'God I love that girl,' he said, shaking his head. 'She'll survive. Things happen.'

'I'm going to the loo,' said Fancy suddenly, and she left.

'I hope I didn't upset her,' George said.

'She's already upset.'

'English women,' George said, 'aren't they fantastic?'

★ ★ ★

He went with Fancy to the hospital for the termination. They were both frightened and they took strength in hiding their fear from each other, determinedly, cheerfully, reassuringly. It was eight a.m. and the waiting room was full of miserable women, a few sheepish men. There were posters for contraceptives everywhere. Eventually, a nurse called Fancy's name – her name really was Fancy, he knew that already. They said goodbye. Peter would come back to pick her up at five, it would be as though she'd spent the day working.

He went to the British Museum and shuffled through the endless rooms, thinking of Roberto when not worrying about Fancy. He stopped in the manuscript room for a while, and in Abyssinian statuary. He got talking to an older museum guard who told him that, contrary to public perception, Japanese tourists were very noisy. 'Canadians all wear those little flags,' he said when Peter told him where he was from. 'Americans do not,' he added. On the way out Peter bought a postcard of a da Vinci drawing that reminded him of Fancy. He had the idea that he would keep it, that he would take it back to Alberta with him and place it between the pages of a notebook and look at it from time to time. On the way out of the museum he realized he would soon be leaving.

He met Fancy at the hospital. The nurse insisted she be delivered to the door in a wheelchair and that he call a taxi. Fancy wanted to go home on the bus, but the nurse stood by, arms crossed, until the taxi arrived. Peter kept asking if she was okay, and she kept saying she was. He took her back to her flat, made her tea, and tried to cosset her, but all she wanted to do was sleep. She said it wasn't too painful; she looked very weak. Peter felt angry and useless. He knew Fancy didn't love him any more – how could she?

He sat by her bed and watched her sleeping; in the middle of the night, he went back to his own flat. He crawled under his ancient pink sheets, exhausted. But he couldn't sleep. In the next room the pigeons were already stirring. After a while, he got up. He went out to the corridor and into the ghost kitchen. When he entered the room the pigeons fled. He tried to sit on the splatter-encrusted chair but it was too broken to support him, so he sat beneath the layered table instead, leaning against the wall. The pigeons began to return slowly. He couldn't see them, it was not yet light, but he could hear them, smell them. They rustled and scrabbled. They made their pigeon noises, that throaty yearning coo. They settled all around him, and he slept.

CHARLIE

Charlie did not like the Royal Family because she did not want to sleep with any of them. Not a one. Not even the little ones. What use was a Royal Family, repository of the nation's fantasies, when you couldn't fancy them? No use at all. Charlie was a republican.

Charlie's mother had named her Charlotte, after Prince Charles. It was better then Andrea, or Edwina, she supposed. Her mother thought Anne too plain. Princess Anne, the one who looks like a horse. The one who is a horse. The only one with any self-respect. A maelstrom of divorce had hit that family. Too bloody rich.

Most of the time, Charlie did not think about that family at all. Sometimes she ran into them, at film previews in Leicester Square, inaugurating hospitals and clinics. They were there, doing their stuff, and Charlie happened by. They'd wave at her in the crowd, and she'd shrug her shoulders. She didn't want any of their waves.

She had to admit it though, she had had sex with Prince Charles a couple of times. It made her bad-tempered just to think of it. It was after his wife Diana had discovered he was still in love with Camilla Parker-Bowles, his old girlfriend. Diana had thrown a frying pan at him, and he'd agreed to stop seeing Camilla. It came out later that he'd had his fingers crossed behind his back, but decided to give Parker-Bowles a wide margin for a while anyway. During these boring, non-love-sexy times, Charles tended to frequent Irish pubs in Camden, a part of north London that smells of beer and rotting vegetables. He travelled incognito, disguised as an Irishman.

Charlie herself went to Irish pubs for the crack, for the music. That night the bar was so crowded she could hardly move. Everyone kept burning each other's hair with their fags. Charlie drank whiskey, and Prince Charles trod on her foot. At the time she didn't know who he was, but she left with him anyway.

He kept on his disguise – a black wig, sideburns, little round dark glasses, and a cool leather hat – and shagged her up against a tree. She made him use a condom, she was paranoid about condoms and carried loads around all the time, and he wasn't too pleased. His fake accent slipped as he came and that was when she realized who he was. She did not have an orgasm, never having liked the Royal Family. And she told him so.

'I've never liked you lot, you know.'

'Sorry?'

'My mum named me after you, but that doesn't mean I've sworn my allegiance or any such thing.'

Prince Charles mumbled something then, Charlie wasn't sure what. She could tell he didn't do this kind of thing often, so she gave him a friendly kick on the tush and sent him on his way. She went back to the pub for lock-up.

The next time she went down the Dog and Bone, he was there again.

'You been here every night, waiting for me?' she asked.

'What're you drinking?' he said, his Irish accent back in place.

They drank together that night, and she was impressed by the way he kept pace with her, not bad for a nancy-boy prince, and she told him so. Her words were garbled though, by the drink, and the music which flowed over their heads in its taps and its paces. The fiddlers were on form tonight, everyone nodding their heads to the rhythm. Sometimes London was a very Irish place.

'Bit different than Buckingham Palace,' she said.

'Too right,' he replied, sounding vaguely Australian. She didn't miss a thing.

That night they shagged up against a different tree. In fact, after the musicians finished, they escaped out of the smoke into the night air and wandered up the road until they reached Hampstead Heath. The Heath whispered sex at night, and as they walked, she noticed men flit in and out of the trees.

'Don't forget your condoms,' she shouted out to them. 'It's a good life, to be a queer boy,' she said to Charles. 'Endless variety.' He didn't reply. They found a tree, and then they found a patch of grass, and they lay together passionately. Charlie liked sex, it was unproblematic. It was all the other business that went along with it that proved so trying. But she and Prince Charles were avoiding unnecessary complications. He rarely spoke, and when he did, Charlie couldn't make sense of anything he said. So she ignored him and offered her body instead.

During the day, nothing much happened. Charlie went to work. Well, she went to look for work. She had lost her job a couple of years ago now, and hadn't been able to find one since. Every day she went to the job centre. But there was never anything there. There was supposed to be a boom on, but for Charlie it was all a big bust. She rolled smaller and smaller cigarettes, and stole books for a living.

She didn't see Prince Charles for a while. In real life, that is; she did see him on the news, he was always on the news, him and that estranged wife of his. Charlie went to her usual haunts. She saw her usual friends, and spoke of usual things. She knew better than to mention shagging the Prince. Bonking the Man Who Would One Day Be King. Without the wig, and the sideburns, and the glasses, and the hat, he was truly ugly.

And then one day she sat down on a bench in St James's Park. The park was near the palace, but she was there to see the ducks. She had been evicted from her flat and couldn't think what else to do with herself. The bailiffs had taken everything, which was okay since it meant she didn't have anything to carry. She sat for a while, the sun was shining, and she raised her face to it. She felt someone sit down beside her.

She looked around. She could smell him. He smelt of greasy hair and leather hat. His black jeans were torn and faded.

'Hi ya,' she said. 'How goes royalty?'

'Fucked if I know,' Prince Charles replied.

'Good,' she said, 'good. Your grasp of the street idiom is improving.'

They sat in companionable silence for a while. Then Prince Charles got up and wandered away, back in the direction of the palace gates. Charlie sat alone. The speeding clouds in the sky slowed their pace.

DEAR ALL

Dear All,

Another year has passed and it's time once again for my annual, up-to-the-minute letter which I send to you all out there. I know some of you feel this is a bit impersonal, but, hey, otherwise you might not hear from me at all. I don't know about you but I really appreciate the letters I get at Christmas.

Well, it's been quite a year for the Mytel family. Larry and I separated and are filing for divorce. This may seem sudden for most of you, especially if you haven't heard from me since my last Christmas letter. We didn't tell anyone until it was all sewn up. In fact, Larry didn't even tell *me* for a couple of years — he waited until just a few weeks before we put together our separation agreement and best of all, he waited until I had someone in place to fill the gap that his departure would have created. That's where Bob comes in. Larry and I had been friends years ago with Bob and his wife Donna. Bob and Donna have since divorced. At a conference in Toronto I ran into Bob. Over the years Larry often told me that he thought I should be married to Bob, not him. And, when we met again at the conference, Bob also seemed to think he was the perfect man for me and went around the cocktail party telling everyone so. I was confused. Where would it all lead? But when Larry started talking 'separation' we both looked to Bob for assistance. And Bob was happy to accommodate us – me. It has worked out really well. Larry has what he wants in his life – to make his own decisions, spend his own money, do his sports, and check out the babes (all the things he wasn't able to do – or rather, wasn't SUPPOSED to be doing while he was with me – because he was married so young). And I have what I want in life – a home, a job, and a man who is loving, caring and protective of me. What a good Christmas this is going to be.

Warren continues reading. He hasn't seen Debbie Barnsley – now Debbie Mytel soon to be Debbie someone else – in sixteen years, but he still gets a photocopied letter from her every year, like minutes from the annual general meeting of a university alumni association. Warren doesn't send Christmas letters. He likes Christmas, he spends it with his wife Kathy and their two kids, but he doesn't send Christmas letters. He receives them though, mostly from distant relatives, school friends, and old girlfriends like Debbie, people he hasn't seen in years. He reads them and, as he reads, he remembers things.

Let me tell you about Bob. He and Brenda didn't have any kids, so their divorce was straightforward, just like Larry and me. He is six foot four (my mother loves that), 185 pounds, with a head full of beautiful silvery-grey hair – handsome, that's the word I'd use. And I do. Often. He owns one 1965 vintage sports jacket which he inherited from his dad, no dress pants, only jeans, Western shirts, tooled leather belts with big silver buckles, cowboy boots and cowboy hats. Otherwise his wardrobe consists of mountain gear. He has lived in town for twenty years. He's a non-smoker, has given up coffee for over four years now, and seldom drinks. He's a great cook and loves to have people over for dinner or to stay the weekend. He leaves for work at seven a.m., comes home to fix me lunch (sometimes we don't make it as far as the kitchen), and returns home after six for nice long evenings. And the sex, well, running the risk of sounding crude, let's just say Bob is a *big* improvement on Larry. We stay in a lot, listen to music, talk, things Larry and I never did.

The down side on Bob: he's poor, but of course, he's very happy as I've heard poor people tend to be. He does all the things I find scary and life-threatening but which he and his ilk think of as 'man-stuff' such as horses, guns, motorcycles, and mountains. Sometimes he's so much like Grandpa I can't believe it. He loves to read which is great, but he tends to have read the entire book and remembered the facts and he corrects me when I'm making eloquent sweeping generalizations. Don't ya loathe it! But it really is love. It is wonderful to love and to be so loved. I am so grateful for the opportunity I've been given to live two terrific lives in one lifetime, my life with Larry and now, my life with Bob.

Warren doesn't do 'man-stuff'. He's surprised to hear Debbie is enjoying that aspect of Bob, she never used to go for macho types. People can change a lot though, especially over the sixteen years since university. Warren himself has changed. He's got two kids for Christ's sake, and he loves his wife, and not only at Christmas. He's happy with his job. He sells real estate on Vancouver Island. Debbie wouldn't believe it if she heard that was what he did now. Or perhaps she would. Perhaps even then, when he was a flamboyant and, he thought, Byronic youth, he had the soul of a real-estate man.

Bob and I plan to have a family. We're not too old, lots of people have families late these days. We feel very settled together and think that we could give a child a good start in life. We just pray (yes, we *pray* – really, both of us – and it is so wonderful to be with a man with whom I can pray) that we will be able to conceive. Hopefully we will have news for you in our next Christmas letter!

My only other big news is that I've been promoted to senior manager level at work. I've been working on a gigantic project which involves data extrapolation from 2500 files from the Chief Medical Examiner's Office, pulling approximately 1200 suicide notes from those files for analysis. The reasons why people kill themselves are very sad indeed, but I've been down myself and I couldn't say I haven't thought about it once or twice. Haven't we all? Bob says he doesn't want me getting any ideas – and who said he didn't have a sense of humour?! If there is one thing I miss about Larry, it is the jokes and the laughter. With Bob I am extremely happy, he just doesn't make me laugh so very much. So let's pray for love AND laughter, for us and for every one of you.

Warren doesn't think he ever met Larry Mytel, he can't quite remember. Nor does he remember Debbie having had a particularly keen sense of humour. Warren isn't much of a joker himself but he likes a laugh. He and his wife Kathy get romantic comedies from the video store. They have a laugh.

Warren wonders what Debbie's job could possibly be. He wonders if Kathy kept Debbie's previous Christmas letters. Maybe if he reads the last decade or so he will be able to figure out where Debbie works. Twelve hundred suicide notes. Phew.

Just then, as Warren sits and stares at Debbie's photocopied letter, Kathy comes into the room.

'What you got there?' she asks.

'Debbie Mytel's Christmas letter.'

'Interesting?'

'Sort of,' says Warren, 'sort of weird. I haven't seen her for sixteen years.'

'Funny how some people like to keep in touch.'

'Yeah,' says Warren. Kathy leaves the room again. She is spending the evening cleaning up after the kids. Once a month she attempts to put everything, all their junk, from all over the house where it belongs, from where it will levitate over the next few weeks. At the same time Warren is meant to go through all the postal paper work, pay the bills, etc. This is part of their deal. Their relationship is one of many deals – Warren takes the kids to school, Kathy picks them up. Warren baby-sits while Kathy is at aerobics, Kathy baby-sits while Warren goes jogging with Al. Warren has sex with Kathy whenever Kathy wants, Warren is always careful to prevent Kathy from conceiving again. Kathy rubs Warren's back when he is tired. They are happy.

Warren would never have been happy with Debbie. Her Christmas letters reassure him of that. They had not been happy even when they were young and had had their – Warren can't bring himself to think of it as an affair even though it went on for some time and it had been nowhere near as solid as the word relationship suggests –

when they were young and had had their . . . thing. It seems such a long time ago. What had they been doing together?

In those days – yes it's true, although Warren can hardly believe it himself any more – in those days, Warren had thought he might be gay. In fact, he had positively longed to be gay. It had seemed the only way of escaping certain inevitabilities. Warren shakes his head – it turned out that the inevitable wasn't so bad after all. He'd had too much Oscar Wilde too early, that must have been the explanation. He and Debbie had met during their first year at university. Everything was wild and strange and confusing. Debbie had developed an enormous crush on Warren. Warren had been bowled over by her. He'd had crushes on other people, plenty of them, all boys. None had ever shown the slightest bit of interest in returning his gaze, but Warren preferred it that way. He kept his crushes secret. Debbie was a different proposition. She was smart, she was pretty in a boyish sort of way. She said she didn't care if he was gay, she wanted him anyway. Debbie believed that this made sense and her logic took his breath away. 'Okay,' he said, finally, 'okay.'

They began doing stuff together – movies, nights in the student union bar drinking with their friends. They went for long walks in the park on frosty mornings. They talked about their families. Warren found himself telling her things he had thought he would never tell anyone. Debbie talked about her friends from high school, how she could never get a date.

They didn't sleep together. Warren avoided that. They kissed several times, on the way home from the bar, when they'd had too much to drink. Warren would drop her off at the door of her residence building, offering up the excuse that he had to get to the library early the next day. She would sigh and turn away. They parted like this over and over again.

But then it seemed he had to decide – he could tell Debbie was getting fed up with him. She didn't say as much, but he saw it in her shoulders, in her face. He realized he didn't want to lose her, not really; he didn't want to be left on his own. He resolved to do the right thing.

They began their evening – that fateful night was how Warren had thought about it even before it happened – in the smoky, beer-soaked student union bar. They got rapidly and thickly drunk. They pretended to discuss Immanuel Kant and then they kissed briefly when the time seemed right. Warren thinks he can still remember the taste of Debbie's mouth from that night – beery, he thinks, wet, female. He almost froze then and there, was almost unable to continue. But something pushed him on, led him back to the halls of residence, that something, of course, being Debbie.

Kathy comes back into the room; she is carrying a small bicycle that belongs to their four-year-old son Teddy. 'What are you doing, Warren?' she asks, slightly suspicious.

'Paying the bills,' says Warren, 'they pile up.' Kathy leaves again. Warren looks back down at Debbie's letter.

And so another year has come to an end. I hope all of you out there have a wonderful Christmas, and that you feel as warmed by happiness as Bob and I do. For those of you I haven't seen for a while, well, I've got a few grey hairs now, but nothing a little dye won't cover up!

Happy New Year!

Love Debbie, reads Warren. Warren never did love Debbie. He never had the opportunity after that fateful night. They went back to her room. Debbie lit all her candles. She loved candles, they were everywhere. Warren had never had sex with anyone before, he didn't know if Debbie had. He hoped she knew what she was doing. They sat on the bed, there was only one chair and it was attached to the desk. Debbie put on a record. Abba. Warren asked her to put on something more serious instead, King Crimson or something like that. He felt a bit woozy from the alcohol. Debbie lay down on the bed and closed her eyes. He lay down too, thinking great, we'll just go to sleep, but he quickly realized that wasn't what she meant him to do.

Debbie looked romantic in the candlelight, even more like a boy than usual, a long-haired Edwardian boy. She was giving instructions. One hand here, the other there. Lips. Teeth. Tongues. Even now Warren can remember his fumbling with embarrassing clarity. They began removing different bits of their clothing, sweaters, shoes. He was surprised by her bra, it looked so . . . architectural. They pushed their bodies together awkwardly, rubbing this, pressing that. They took off their jeans. Underwear. Everything seemed damp, slippery. Debbie wanted Warren to lie on top of her, so he did, feeling heavy, unwieldy, trying not to burp. Debbie had stopped wiggling and was lying very still. She looked up at him, her young face full of expectation, desire and fear. In her eyes he saw the future, kids, cars, summer holidays. He knew what he was supposed to do next.

'I can't,' he said, rearing back, elbowing Debbie in the stomach, bashing his own head against the wall. 'I don't know why, I just can't.' Warren is speaking out loud now, in his own sitting room.

'Why not?' says Kathy who has returned with an armful of books. Warren looks up.

'Nothing hon,' he says, embarrassed again. She smiles as she crosses the room.

Later, when he and Debbie had their clothes back on and were drinking cups of tea, Warren still apologizing and Debbie still on the edge of tears, Debbie had said, 'They have clubs for people like you.'

'What?' said Warren.

'You know, the gay students' club, things like that.'

'Oh?' said Warren.

'You don't always have to feel outcast and disgusting.'

'Oh,' says Warren. 'Thanks.'

Kathy comes back into the room. This time her arms are empty. She walks right up to Warren, plucks Debbie's Christmas letter out of his hands and pushes the dining room table back a couple of feet. She places herself unceremoniously on Warren's lap. The weight of her body brings Warren swiftly through the years. He puts his arms around her waist. He remembers that Kathy used to look like a boy, before she had the kids. He says to himself it's not my fault about Debbie and Larry and Bob. Kathy leans back against his chest.

'Maybe we should do a Christmas letter next year,' she says.

'Oh yeah, what would we say?' asks Warren. 'Dear All. Everything is exactly the same this year as it was last year except we're all one year older. We divorced and remarried in the spring. The children share the psychological profile of a serial killer. For those of you who haven't seen me in sixteen years, I've aged well, I now look exactly like Marlon Brando. For those of you that Kathy and I never slept with, well, you don't know what you're missing. Merry Christmas. Love Warren and Kathy.' Warren stops.

'Debbie Mytel,' said Kathy, picking up the letter. 'Did you sleep together?'

'Not really,' says Warren. 'Hardly at all.'

THE VISITS ROOM

Every time I visit James in prison he tries to have sex with me. The visits room is crowded, overheated in winter, airless in summer. We are allowed to sit on the same side of the table. We start by holding hands, we progress to kissing, he places one hand on my breast. It makes him die, I can feel it, he would give everything away if he could just have me. Before I come to visit I get a letter from him; he tells me not to wear any knickers, to wear a big, long skirt. To sit on his lap, my skirt covering us, and then to move in a slow way that will let him get inside me.

We never quite make it. An officer always walks by just when I think it's about to happen, and they always make a joke about us trying to have sex and James always denies it and gets angry and I slide off his lap and back onto the chair next to his. Once the officer goes past James always, always, looks as though he is going to cry. But he never does. And neither do I.

James killed his brother-in-law. It is an unalterable fact. Bobby was a violent man. We knew he used to hurt James' sister Maria. It wasn't straightforward slapping around, we knew he tortured her, the marks on her body showed us. Finally, after years of it, Maria threw Bobby out. James was relieved, we all were. We thought a happy ending had arrived.

But then Maria came round one Sunday. She looked terrible, her hair a wild mess, her face bruised and scratched. Weeping, she told us that Bobby had broken into the house and raped her, and gone off with their two kids. As she spoke I felt James' body grow tense. He had an idea of where Bobby had gone, I don't know how. So James went round to try and get the kids back, and they got into a fight, and James killed Bobby. He crushed his skull with a heavy old mirror that Bobby's new girlfriend had hanging on the wall. He drove Maria's kids to our place. Maria was happy to see her children, but I could tell something had gone wrong. James turned towards the front door again. I asked him where he was going. 'To the police,' he said, and I knew what had happened.

James was in prison on remand for a long time. When his trial finally took place we realized he would lose. We hoped for a verdict of manslaughter. He had no previous convictions, he had never been in trouble before. But they said he had gone round intending to kill Bobby, and I guess he had. He was convicted of murder and got life. He was given a life sentence.

The visits room is very bare. The tables and chairs are battered and old, the walls are grey, the barred Perspex windows are filthy. An officer sits at a table on a raised platform. We are watched. Other prisoners have noisy, sociable visits but James and I often sit in silence. It is difficult to talk; I feel that James has himself only barely held in. When I'm there he will sit and clutch my hand and stare into my eyes for the whole two hours we are allowed together. He would never have done that outside.

I brought my sister Maureen to see James one day. At the next table another lifer, a young, good-looking lad, was being visited by his family. I saw him looking at Maureen, and she noticed too. They got to talking, we pushed our tables closer. James and I held hands while Maureen had a laugh with Ian. Now Maureen goes to visit Ian on her own. She says thirteen to sixteen years seems like a long time to wait for a man. She laughs and says how can you know you love someone without being able to fuck them? And then she blushes and looks at me and says she is sorry. I don't care. It's good to have someone to make the journey to visits with.

James tells me that Ian is a nice lad. He killed a woman during the course of a burglary. He was sixteen and he was not expecting anyone to be home. He graduated from young offenders' prison to adult prison a few years back. James says Ian was just a burglar and never meant anyone any harm. James is changing; before, he would have rattled his newspaper and said he thought boys like Ian should be strung up.

The visits room is not a good place to conduct a marriage. It is not a good place for anything except smoking and drinking cups of tea. James and I got married when we were both twenty-four, old enough and not that young any more. We were happy to be married, we felt we belonged together. We used to have a good time with flying diaphragms, mucking up with spermicide, condoms that refused to unroll. Then we decided to have a child and we binned all the birth control. But no luck. I thought we should go to the doctor and get some help, see where the problem lay, but James didn't want to. He said we should just keep on having sex, and if I got pregnant that was good, but otherwise it was not meant to be. He said he didn't want to find out if it was his fault, or mine, something gone wrong inside one of us, something sour, barren, unfit. This way we are in it together, it is no one else's business, and I suppose, in a way, he is right.

Now that James is in prison I'm glad we don't have children. It would have made it all much worse. In the visits room the children often cry, and their upsets make it harder for the adults, I can see that. There is a little roped-off area where volunteers play with the kids while their mothers spend some time with the dads. Someone has tried to make it cheery, but they haven't succeeded. The wall murals look gruesome, the plastic toys dirty.

I brought James' sister Maria to the prison once. It wasn't a good visit. Maria cried the whole time, she went on and on about her fatherless children, about being on her own, about how much she misses Bobby. I was stunned. James is her brother. I would not have brought her if I knew she would say that. James sat pushed back in his chair with a completely blank expression on his face while Maria's despair rolled over him in waves. You killed my husband, she said, plain as day, everyone sipping their tea and laughing together in the crowded, smoky, hot, visits room. James said nothing, but I could see him harden, I could see him drying out and stiffening in his chair. Maria's voice got louder and louder. You murdered my husband, she said again and again. I couldn't listen to any more: I hit her, I slapped her across the face. She stopped talking, stopped sobbing, and just sat there on the filthy, lop-sided metal chair. I looked up and saw the officer watching us, a look of contempt and disgust on his face. Two bitches and a murderer and their sordid argument. At that moment I wished we all three were dead.

Last month I was invited to go to the prison for a Lifer Family Day. I received a leaflet in the post, inviting me. There would be speakers talking about life sentences and the system for lifers, there would be time for both inmates and their families to ask questions. There would be an opportunity to have lunch with James. A whole day together, an entire day spent sitting in the visits room. The leaflet said it was a hard-won opportunity and not to be missed.

We are allowed two visits per month if I go on the weekend, four if I can get there on weekdays although that's difficult. The Lifer Family Day would not be counted against our visits. I saw James a few weeks before and I asked him if he thought I should bring his parents, perhaps his brother William who still talks about trying to mount an appeal. James said no, he was looking upon it as a chance to spend time with me. I could not help it, but part of me was filled with dread. A whole day in that room, a whole day of being next to James but no chance to be with him. Of course I agreed to go, I sent in my name, and I travelled up to the prison first thing that day.

When I arrived the visits room was already crowded. The tables we usually sat at had been pushed to one side and rows of seats were arranged in a large semi-circle. There was an overhead projector and a lectern and a number of men in suits. I found a chair in the back row. We heard the keys and keychains rattling and the prisoners' door opened and James and the other men came through. When he saw me he smiled and I felt the same searing pain that I always do. Sometimes I dream that when I leave the visits room James comes with me. We are outside in the fresh air, and the flowers, and the breeze.

James sat down beside me. The speakers started speaking, putting diagrams up on the overhead projector, explaining how a life sentence is served. The basic principle is that everything takes a very long time. The average length currently served is 15.4 years, but some men are in for much longer. Years in one institution are followed by years in another institution. In between there are one or two meetings. The speakers used words like sentence planning, sentence review, even probation once or twice. It was very absorbing for the first hour. James kept one hand on my knee and the other around my waist and when I looked at him his face seemed younger, more serene. We had a tea break. Maureen was there along with Ian's family, so we got together and had a chat. James was talkative, relaxed, nearly effusive. He told one or two stories. The speakers started up again, and then it was time for lunch.

It was wonderful to eat with James again. I had not seen him eat for such a long time; we had not eaten a meal together since he had left for the police station that day. Someone had gone to a lot of trouble over the food, there were sandwiches, bits of pie, pastries and cake. The mood in the visits room was slightly euphoric, everyone piled their plates high. Ian's brother fetched us pitchers of water, pots of tea. It was like being at a banquet, it was like our wedding all over again. James smiled and ate, and then smiled with food in his teeth. He kept one arm around me. I fed him triangles of sandwiches. We toasted the table with our mugs.

In the afternoon, the speakers started up again. The overhead projector went on, and one of the deputy governors began to talk. The room had become warmer still. People had urgent questions, lots of hands were waving, prisoners argued their side passionately. But in the back row where James and I were sitting it was a different story. In the back row couples were kissing. We had eaten together and now we wanted more.

I got onto James' lap, like I had done countless other times. He buried his face in my shirt, opening one or two buttons with his teeth. I could smell him and beneath his prison smell of tobacco and staleness, there was the smell of James. I couldn't believe what was happening. There were no officers strolling up and down the aisles, we were as far away from an officer as we had ever been. I smoothed my skirt and kept my face turned forward so I at least looked as though I was listening. James fumbled, and it was awkward, I had to lift my weight from one leg to another. But then – I had to turn, I had to bend slightly, it was a bit painful – it happened. I could hear James trying to control his breathing. A few heads turned, and quickly faced away again. I felt him, I felt it all, it was piercing and complete. James buried his face in my back and bit me hard instead of crying out.

I slid off his lap. Our smell was drowned by cigarettes, food and sweat. There were disapproving glances, but I didn't care. This was all we had to hope for, this was all we would get. The afternoon ended, James held me tight in his arms, and I left.

I know that it is wrong to kill. I know that Bobby should not have died. James is in prison now, we are paying for

Bobby's death. It is a huge debt, and his sentence is very long. But James is just James and I am his wife and the visits room is our asylum.

BLACK TAXIS

Shelagh sleeps in the place where black taxis park for the night. Side by side in long, straight rows, the taxis wait for ignition, for their engines to lurch, diesel-filled, into action. They perch like blackbirds on a telephone wire, anticipating, silent. Shelagh waits with them. She is hungry.

Late at night in London when King's Cross Station has become too inhospitable Shelagh creeps into the old security box, unmanned and abandoned now there are video cameras. She clutches her breasts under her thick, dirty coat and sleeps like a child. Shelagh never used to be good at sleeping just anywhere but now she could sleep in the middle of Oxford Street if she had to, calmed by the sound of moving taxis.

In London the pavements are crowded with people trying to get a decent night's sleep. A blanket and a doorway, basic human rights. Walking down Kingsway is like being an intruder in a giant dormitory. The Strand — a beach along the Thames before landfill, concrete and shops — is dotted with people lying out, fishing for food and money. Shelagh sees them when she goes walking.

The security box behind King's Cross Station is as good as any to spend the night. A drunken taxi driver might wander by hoping to grab a few hours' rest on the passenger seat of his vehicle. Shelagh might catch him off guard, she might creep up on him, surprise him. Or he might invite her into the cab himself. This is Shelagh's ambition. She wants to spend the night inside one of the dark taxis. She longs to stretch her body out along the black leather seat once again, she wants that luxury, that space, that engine power. If she had the money she would pay to be driven through the night streets of London while she slept on the passenger seat. If she had the money Shelagh would live in the back of a cab while an impersonal stranger drove her from bridge to bridge, station to station.

No one sees Shelagh come or go from her hiding place; no one looks for her. She went missing from her life six months ago. She is presumed not living. Her friends divided up her possessions; there was only one minor argument over who would get the stereo. Shelagh does not wonder what happened to her stuff, in fact, she does not care. She is not interested in stuff any more.

At night there is no better sight than a black cab in the dark, slick streets of London. Black taxis are not simply cars, not just wheels and seats, but strong and purring creatures. As they slide by under the yellow streetlights it's as though they actually breathe London's diesel air, full lungs under their metal shells, like a new breed of nuclear-age insect, parasites within a city-host. Shelagh thinks taxis can take her places where she has never been, she thinks they might show her new ways. Black taxis know the streets of London like Underground trains know the tunnels that lie below. They slip through the streams of traffic like water through mud, tide across sand. Shelagh believes the soul of London hides beneath the bonnet of a rain-wet, shining taxi. She crouches in the car park and looks out across the slumbering rows.

King's Cross sits, smoky and steamy, festering malevolently beneath its spruced-up façade. Its mean heart still throbs, people still sleep unprotected on its platforms, in the sidings, the places where disused trains wait. Shelagh used to think that nothing could be more dangerous than sleeping on the hard ground in a public place, each breath an act of faith, I trust I'll be alive in the morning. Shelagh does not think about trust any more. She thinks about keeping warm.

In the station crowds of passengers queue for taxis under the shelter of an overhang. They come off their trains and wait patiently, bags and parcels piled beside them. The cabs swoop down, their yellow signs beckoning. Shelagh wanders by not noticing the rubbish, the food packaging, the discarded newspapers, the smashed bottles and pools of sick. She gazes up into the filthy glass vaulting of the roof of the station and watches the pigeons fly to and fro. Trains pull in, people run for trains just pulling out, but Shelagh is not interested in trains. They stick to the rails, they don't weave, they don't flow down Pall Mall like lava. Shelagh pays no heed, she is staring upwards, a ray of grey light illuminating her face. She is listening for something. She is listening for something to rise over and above the noise of London. She is waiting for ignition, like a taxi itself.

When Shelagh sleeps in the abandoned security box she dreams she arrives by taxi. She dreams of being driven. She arrives and arrives and arrives. The taxi door opens and she gets out. The taxi door closes and she is driven away. The taxi takes a steep corner. The taxi pulls away from the kerb. She turns and waves. In her dreams Shelagh always travels by taxi. A black cab is always waiting for her.

Sometimes Shelagh dreams of his arrival. He comes by taxi. The cab pulls into the car park and stops next to the security box. The door swings open. Shelagh stands, pulling her coat around herself. She steps forward and climbs in.

Inside it is dark. It is warm and smells fetid, like an unaired bedroom. She can hear him breathing. He pulls her close as the cab moves away. He pushes her down onto the black leather seat. Shelagh feels his lips on her cheek, his teeth on her neck, his hands on her body. His fingers are cool like leather. The cab circles around King's Cross Station, circling and circling, Pancras Road, York Way, Pancras Road, York Way. She can hear her own heart pounding.

Later, he takes her back to the security box. The door swings open and Shelagh slowly climbs out of the cab. She closes the door and he is driven away. She feels tired. She settles down inside the security box after looking to see how many taxis she has for company. The cabs remind her of him; they make her wait easier. He might take her away with him forever next time.

It is a kind of lie, the life Shelagh lives, a prostitution or addiction, a junkie's life. But this agony is what she is after, it is what she left everything for, it is what she wants. Only when he comes in his taxi does she feel truly happy. Only in that dark, decaying dimness does she feel strong and whole.

The first time she saw him he arrived by taxi. She still had a job then, a flat, an ordinary life. She began to dream of being out on the streets late at night, in the rain, alone. In these dreams she was waiting for something. She ached for it to come. One night, after having been at a party, she found herself standing on a street corner in the rain, alone. While she shivered a taxi pulled up in front of her. Its yellow light was on. She climbed in but was not by herself. He was there, she could smell his somehow familiar scent. She felt the black leather seat under her palms as she allowed herself to be taken.

The second time was several months later. She had almost forgotten, but not quite. It was early evening, windy, a bit wet. She was standing on Piccadilly waiting for the light to change. The pavement and street were crowded. Buses and cars formed a honking queue. She was tired, her back ached from sitting at her desk. She carried a bag full of shopping.

A taxi pulled up in front of her very close to the kerb. The door swung open and for a moment she felt cross, thinking someone was going to get out and block her way just as the lights changed. But then the smell drifted out from inside. She bent down to take a closer look. The smell grew stronger, drawing her in. The door closed behind her and the cab moved forward through the pedestrians, cyclists, and other taxis. He was with her, she could sense, if not see, him.

The third time was several weeks later, the fourth time only one or two weeks after that. Soon she was being picked up every day. Always after work, in the dark, off the pavement. Shelagh did not alter her work day in any way – she left for the office in the morning and left for home in the evening. But somewhere between A and B, B and C, the taxi would come, the door would swing open, and she would climb in.

Inside the cab was always the same. He was always there, smelling of blood and leather. She believed she was the only one he favoured.

When the drive was over, the cab door would swing

open and she would climb out, always at exactly the same place, King's Cross Station. She would get out and no one would notice. She would stumble home. During the day her body ached with longing; at night she fell asleep with the sound of the diesel-powered engines in her ears.

Shelagh stopped performing well at work. She began coming in late and then later still, not caring what anyone thought. Eventually, she was sacked. On that day she put on her coat and walked to King's Cross Station where she stood and waited. He did not come. She stood and waited all night, fending off other men in other, inferior, cars. The streets grew very dark and then light again, until it was so light that she knew he would not appear. She slept on the concourse of the station all day, and stood on Pentonville Road as night fell. He did not come then either. In the middle of the night she grew tired and hailed a taxi on her own. When the driver asked her where she wanted to go she said she did not know. He made her get out and she watched as he drove around the back of the station. That was how she found the black cab hotel and that was when she settled down to wait.

Now Shelagh waits to be driven away. She would accept an empty cab but prefers one with him in it, one reeking of him, redolent of his grave-dirt perfume. He is everything she has ever wanted in a man, more than a man and somehow less, both heart-beating with life and long dead. Without him her life is drained of meaning, as drained as she becomes once she has been with him. He arrives by taxi, leaves by taxi, and does not exist for her otherwise.

A KIND OF DESIRED
INVASION

S tarting with the Belgian chocolates, desire seemed
a potent and dynamic force, like a nuclear engine,
high-powered and probably lethal. The chocolates
made her melt, sticky, gooey, and desire made her
harden, glass blown by fire. She flexed her muscles and
felt strong and American, like an airforce base in a foreign
country. Strength, however, was not part of the problem.

He, of course, was a married man, a married Englishman, like Trevor Howard or James Mason in an early
role. Beneath his pale exterior something burnt and
melted, hardened then softened. She could tell this by
looking at his back as he stood at the bar ordering more
drinks. His long neck was tinged a bright pink as though
reflecting some internal glow. He had just given her the
chocolates and she had kissed him. After their lips parted,
he sank into the tatty, beer-stained seat, then suddenly
stood, knocking his knees on the edge of the table. She
felt she had shocked him and his response was to wing
slightly out of control.

The colour of his neck faded as he returned to the table
with the drinks. They were colleagues at the university.
She was not married. She was new to the country and did

not have many friends. It was not like her to flirt with married Englishmen. Her sexual habits had changed with the times and, besides, in England all the signifiers were different. Here the semiotics of sexuality were not her own.

Like celibacy, chocolates seemed an old-fashioned gesture, from another time although perfectly appropriate somehow. Perhaps romance had snuck back into vogue, she thought, along with sexual caution. Chocolates, especially European ones, were decadent and luxurious, like love letters and long kisses, something one's parents had before they married. Soft-centred milk chocolates that came as one bit them were almost as exciting as dancing with someone you knew you were about to sleep with used to be.

His marriage to another woman, an immutable fact, posed even greater restrictions on their fledgling nuclear romance. Infidelity had become freshly dangerous, potentially much more lethal to a marriage than previously. Restraint carried with it nobility, safety, a new kind of self-respect.

'Would you like another chocolate?' she asked, leaning against his shoulder. His leather jacket smelt raw, his jeans felt soft and worn. He was dressed like an American, it was she who looked English in her patched tweed jacket and jodhpurs. She looked horsy as well as strong, like a kind of repellent 'Country Living' housewife. But her clothes were not literal, as clothes rarely are; she was as much a bloodsportswoman as he was a baseball fan. Still, he was married, even if he didn't look it. What do married people look like?

'Let's go away for the weekend,' he said.

'What about your wife?'

'She can stay home. I'll say it's work.'

'She won't believe you. It's such a cliché.' They paused and gulped their drinks, anticipating courage from the alcohol. 'Anyway, what would we do?' she asked. 'Play chess?'

'No. We'd go for long walks and eat hot meals and watch the sunset. We'd kiss with the wind in our faces. I'd hold you close and feel your heartbeat.' He placed a chocolate under his tongue and waited for it to melt down.

She looked at him longingly, wondering if he really did want to have an affair with her. She had a theory that English men enjoyed sex even less than her male compatriots. She was allowed to like it, wasn't she? Maybe this new restraint appealed to most people, perhaps everyone felt more comfortable with prudishness.

'I want to look at you without any clothes on,' she said suddenly as she watched him suck his chocolate. His neck began to glow again. He moaned softly. 'I want to see you naked.' The people at the next table moved their chairs forward imperceptibly. He closed his eyes and leaned back. 'I want to run my hands down the length of your legs. Both of them. One at a time.' He moaned more loudly and the people at the next table held their drinks in mid-air. She pressed against the seat, her hands between her own legs. The lights in the pub flickered like a fluttering heart, a clenching and rumbling nervous gut.

After a while he stopped shaking and bit into another chocolate. Its softness covered his teeth, coating his tongue. In a voice thick with sugar and lust he said, 'You are driving me wild. I don't understand you.'

'What?' she said.

'You are so foreign and yet so familiar. Like sex itself, I guess, a kind of desired invasion.'

They fucked like chickens, their feathers ruffled, pecking and scratching at nothing, everything. She grappled with him as he pushed against her, shoving him away and urging him on. He tried to be controlled, even a bit leisurely, but as he pulled back he could not help but rush forward again. He felt the condom tear inside her. It was all he could do to stop.

'It broke,' he said.

'Shit.'

'Is there another?'

'Over here somewhere.' She crawled away and scrabbled through the junk on the bedside table, returning with another foil-wrapped package. 'Let's try again.'

They had been fucking like this for a few months, slyly, without letting on to the outside world. They would meet in her flat – the weekend away was still talked about although not realized. He would arrive at her door and they would begin right away, sometimes before he took his coat off. They did not talk much, what was there to say? She saw more than enough in the guilt and pleasure on his face to make questions redundant.

It would not go anywhere; there was nowhere for it to go. She could not take him back to America with her, he could not take her home. They had sex protected from each other, the little slip of rubber a true barrier made of caution and sensibility. Because of it they simply could not plunder on ahead without thinking. They always had to pause and reflect.

'In my country,' she began like a student from abroad, 'the English are often thought as as fey.'

'Humph. In my country,' he mocked her slightly, 'Americans are often thought of as vulgar.'

'How fey.'

He pushed harder today, knowing he would not hurt her. When he came he pulled away quickly so as not to spill his bodily fluids, like the instructions on the box of condoms said.

She reminded him of somebody from a movie, maybe it was Kathleen Turner in *Body Heat*, sometimes Sharon Stone in *Basic Instinct*. Not an old movie star but someone contemporary and less defined, whose face resembled that of a dozen different actresses. He, too, relied on clichés for guidance, for cross-cultural understanding. He thought he would like to be more like her; when she spoke, people listened. The twang in her vowels commanded attention. And he watched as she capitalized on this, she saw where it could be to her advantage to be perceived as a celluloid creation.

Some afternoons they talked at cross-purposes; it was not just their vocabularies that differed. He would appear cold and withdrawn, tormented with guilt over his wife. She would become overly effusive in response, feeling hopelessly alone. 'Are you mad?' she would ask abruptly, meaning 'Are you angry?'

'No,' he would reply, thinking she was implying he was mad – insane – with desire for her (which, in a way, he was). Then they would thrash out their anxieties in bed, moaning and coming to false understandings.

Two cultures rarely comprehend each other, especially when one is waxing and the other waning. The weaker needs to copy the stronger – for every one of her foreign

73

bombing campaigns conducted with supreme arrogance and ruthless certainty he had his own dirty little war on distant barren islands, his own vicious murder on the Rock. Were they playing out these scenarios in sex? Did he want to be dominated?

One night he put a Belgian chocolate inside her and as it melted he licked away the cream. 'Do they have Marmite in America yet?' he asked.

She broke off mid-moan to reply, 'We'll never have Marmite over there. It's you who'll get peanut butter over here. That's the way it works.' She was coated with chocolate as he pushed inside her once again.

His marriage seemed like the Atlantic Ocean to her, something vast and unknowable which she could not attempt to bridge but only fly over at a terrible speed. It kept them apart, kept them foreign to each other, him unhaveable, her unhad.

After a year his wife still appeared not to have noticed the smell of another woman on her husband's face. He was always careful to wash his chiselled visage, of course, but in a year of passion one would think some small scent would have escaped, a tracking odour that would put her senses on alert. It was time for the Other Woman to go back to America. Her academic job had run its course. She had found England a cold place. The rooms where she lived were damp, even while the brief summer had flickered. Her career beckoned, the Atlantic Ocean dimmed and became crossable. And yet, there was the problem of her married Englishman. Would she simply leave him behind? Would she just move away and forget?

One afternoon in bed in her flat she said, 'I will be leaving soon, you know.'

He sat up, surprised. 'I thought you had the afternoon free.'

'I do. It's the rest of the time I'm talking about. I have to go home.'

'I thought you liked it here, I thought you thought it was fun living in England and sleeping with me.'

'I do. But I can't be a tourist forever.'

They argued about it for the rest of the afternoon, he becoming sullen and sorry, she remaining dispassionate, untouched. She was impressed by his sudden remorse. She had always felt insulated from pain with him, as if the condoms served to forever prevent them from getting unhealthily close. Now he was filling their relationship with a seriousness she had always assumed it could not possibly contain.

'Don't you think,' he began to plead, 'that sleeping together automatically provides us with a kind of contract?'

'A legal document? Fucking gives us certain rights over each other? I fuck you therefore I owe you?'

'You can be so crude sometimes,' he said as though wounded.

'It's in my blood,' she replied.

'I think your blood runs a bit cold,' he said.

'You are the one who is married,' she said, 'not me. I know what that means. I know what married people look like.'

'Huh?' he said, like an American. 'What do married people look like?'

She paused and then smiled and said, 'They wear rings on their fingers. They have ties around their hearts. They love their wives and will never leave them.'

'Oh,' he said sadly, and they both knew she was right. They would exchange chocolates and sex for sweet memories. And that would be the end of it.

MY LIFE AS A GIRL IN A MEN'S PRISON

I can feel myself changing at night. Alone, in my cell – it's such a cliché, but it's true, it is my actual situation. I live in a cell in a closed unit, in a prison within a prison; but at night I feel the changes taking place and this is something that no one – not even me – can control. And they are letting me get away with it, they are letting me do it, which is the astounding thing. They, the authorities – another cliché, I know – can't stop me now, it's too late.

Like Esmerelda the English teacher, Kelsey lives in London; that is, he lived in London before *it* happened. *It* is what Kelsey calls the accident, the event, the thing that happened that got Kelsey locked away. Another queer-bashing gone wrong – Kelsey ended up the murderer instead of the murderee – in old London Town, under the shadow of the gleaming, phallic Canary Bird building. 'The Canary's stopped singing,' Kelsey used to say to John in the kitchen after those Canadian business brothers went bankrupt. 'Oh,' he would continue, looking out the window of their flat, 'I hate that fucking thing.' Secretly this was not true; Kelsey and John rather admired the colossus. It made them think about what it might be like to live in New

York, far away from the grimiest end – the grimy east end – of a filthy old city.

Now Kelsey lives in prison, but Esmerelda the English teacher lives in the city. She works in the prison and for her it is part of London; she travels there on a bus down the long, bereft, empty-shop-windows high street. But Kelsey and the other inmates on his wing are not in the city any longer, not in the world any longer in fact. They are in the closed wing, the segregation unit, on Rule 43: they are the nonces, the sex beasts, the scum.

Esmerelda teaches English in the prison; she was made redundant when the Putney secondary school where she worked was amalgamated with a secondary school in Tooting. Tooting – nothing to toot about there as far as she could see. Esmerelda misses teaching teenage girls, she misses the single-sex environment of the secondary girls' school. The prison is, of course, a single-sex environment also, but the other sex, the opposite one, men. And yet there is Kelsey, Kelsey who is neither here nor there, neither one nor the other; perhaps Esmerelda's nostalgia for girls is part of the reason why she finds herself drawn to Kelsey now.

London is full of prisons; Esmerelda discovered this when she began working in one. They are part of the unseen, unnoticed structure of the city like Underground ventilation shafts and sewers. Spot one and you start seeing them everywhere. Wormwood Scrubs – oh, the very name makes Esmerelda shudder. Holloway. Pentonville. Wandsworth. Brixton. Brrr.

The masculinity of the place is palpable; the air is thick with maleness. Esmerelda thinks she can actually feel it on her skin. The prison smells like a huge locker room that somehow ended up inside an even larger greasy spoon, sweat and socks mixed with custard and frying mince. And tobacco – a dense fogbank of cigarette smoke builds up during the course of the day. They all smoke, all the men, every single one of them, except Kelsey. Kelsey somehow manages to remain nicotine-free, sweetened.

There are twenty of us in this unit, twenty of us lowest of the low, a layer of scum twenty men thick. They're not so bad, the others. I don't mind them. We're just a little misunderstood. Well, actually, we're massively misunderstood, in fact, none of us understands it ourselves really. But we get on okay, we watch each other's backs to a certain extent; it's all right so long as no one from out there can get to us with their home-made weapons, 'shanks' – bent nails, metal chair legs, etc. They're all so butch out there in the open wings, it's frightening; but butch is the wrong word, those kinds of words don't work in here.

Esmerelda goes down to the segregation unit once a week to teach an English class. Kelsey doesn't come to her class yet, but Esmerelda has been told about him by an officer and by a governor grade as well. 'He likes to iron, does our Kelsey,' said the Governor. 'He irons everything down there in the seg unit. Ironed shirts, ironed socks, they even have bloody ironed sheets down there. And it's weird,' he continued while Esmerelda smiled and nodded, 'Kelsey is changing. Right before our very eyes, he is changing. His hair is different now and, well,' the Governor paused, his eyes looking beyond the bars for the right word, 'it's uncanny, really, it is.'

The other men in the seg unit did not discuss Kelsey, and Esmerelda did not ask questions about him. The other men – mostly rapists, child abusers, and paed-ophiles – were reading Thomas Hardy and the class held long discussions about fate that Esmerelda found fascinating. Fate seemed to be something they knew about; fate and coming to a bad end. They engaged with Hardy on a completely different level than teenaged school girls, and this made Esmerelda read Hardy differently as well. When she was in prison Esmerelda found the rest of her life faded away, as though life started and finished at the prison gates. London was not really out there at all, the prison floated somewhere in outer space.

Outside the closed unit, in the Education block and on the open wings, things were not quite so extreme. One of her students, a man who could recite Coleridge's 'The Ancient Mariner' in its entirety – a lifetime's work – described his cell to her as part of an oral exam one day. 'And I have a view,' he concluded.

'What?' said Esmerelda.

'From the top of B-Wing, where my cell is, I have a view. I can see London from up there. I can see some council flats, some garages, and the back of the high street.'

Esmerelda smiled appreciatively. 'That's London all right,' she said.

'You don't know what a relief it is,' he continued, 'to know that while I'm stuck in here, out there people are hanging up their laundry.'

'Ahh, London,' said another man, 'I miss it. I miss the dirty old town. Brilliant, isn't it? Where do you live, miss?'

'Archway,' replied Esmerelda.

'Ahh, the big old arch over Highgate Road. What I

wouldn't do for a ride in a taxi under that just now,' the prisoner sighed. 'Highgate Cemetery – I've got my plot sorted already.'

'Oh?' said Esmerelda. 'Speaking of plots –' and she brought Thomas Hardy back into the conversation.

When Kelsey came to Esmerelda's seg unit English class for the first time he walked in smelling of roses, St James's Park summer roses, Esmerelda thought. He took a seat alongside the other men. He had very curly, blond long hair, blue blue eyes, full pouting lips, and bad skin. 'I'm sorry I've missed the first few classes, miss,' he said politely. 'I had prior engagements.'

The other men smirked. 'Oh, so you're engaged now are you, Kelsey?' one of them asked.

'No,' said Kelsey, a kind of Princess Diana at a charity dinner smile across his face, 'but I am terribly, awfully, busy.'

Esmerelda needed a few moments to recover from the impact of Kelsey's entrance. Her silence was filled by the other prisoners; they always had plenty to say. Kelsey gazed at Esmerelda, she could feel his steady eyes upon her. 'Where'd you get your shoes, miss?' he asked eventually, as though they were the only people in the room.

'Covent Garden.'

'Oh that dump,' he replied, smiling.

The class went on, Esmerelda's composure returned. Kelsey had done all the reading, and he was smart; she could see he would be a good student. They finished on time and the other men got up to leave, the sound of banging trays and officers shouting. Kelsey walked up to where Esmerelda was sitting on the edge of a table. He leaned over and whispered, 'I've got an English degree.' His breath smelt of mint.

Esmerelda turned towards him. 'What are you doing studying for a GCSE?'

'Boredom, you see. I'd rather talk about Thomas Hardy than mop floors all day. And besides, I heard you were nice. There's not a lot of women around here, you might have noticed. It's important to make the most of every opportunity.'

Esmerelda left the prison at 4:30 that afternoon. Outside workers, education people, probation, psychology, left at the same time every day. After that the prison fell silent for a moment before the evening racket began. As she left Esmerelda imagined Kelsey in his cell; as she left Kelsey imagined Esmerelda on her way home. He stood on his bed and looked out his cell window into the tiny seg exercise yard. It was raining and the London sky was very low. Kelsey had a theory, one he used to expound upon with his lover John, that the reason there were so few skyscrapers in London was that in the winter the sky was too low. 'There's hardly room for a five-storey block of flats,' he'd say looking out the kitchen window as he did the washing-up, 'let alone a sky-scraper. The Canary Bird has completely disappeared today.'

Esmerelda took the bus home. That evening she stayed in by herself and watched TV. The milk had gone sour so she ate her bowl of cereal dry. The phone did not ring. As she cleaned her face to get ready for bed she remembered Kelsey's skin; it must be the hormones, she thought, although she didn't know why, no one had said anything about hormones.

Which am I: a nonce, a sex beast, or scum? Hmm. Nonce

maybe, that seems the most likely. Perhaps I should change my name to Nancy when the time comes. Nance, I'll be used to that. In here I'm just Kelsey, of course, number LV0125 – yet another cliché. I'll have to write a book when I get out: My Life as A Girl in a Men's Prison.

I'll have to write a book, thought Esmerelda before she went to sleep: *My Life as A Girl in a Men's Prison.*

Later that week when Esmerelda was getting ready to go teach her seg unit English class, she found herself staring in the bathroom mirror. A new haircut, she thought, that's what I need. A new face. A complete new body. She ran her fingers through her hair and put on more make-up than usual.

In class the men were noisy and reluctant to work. Kelsey came in late, wearing a neck-scarf that appeared to have been torn from a prison sheet. When Esmerelda glanced from his neck to his face she found he was looking at her. Kelsey shrugged and smiled apologetic-ally, 'A girl's got to make some attempt, doesn't she?' The other men hissed and jeered half-heartedly. Es-merelda blushed. The class continued.

The weeks went by. The season changed in its oblique London way. In prison time passes like water in the Thames, slow, murky, inevitable, taking forever to get to the sea. Kelsey missed his lover John. John missed Kelsey. Kelsey felt he had been wrongly convicted and sentenced. These are things suitable for understatement only.

Esmerelda continued to teach English. She gave assignments. Her classes worked towards taking their exams. Kelsey continued to change. One day Esmerelda thought she could see a hint of breasts beneath his carefully pressed prison shirt. Kelsey came up to her after class, in the few moments before the officers came to shoo everyone away. 'I'm worried,' he said.

'What about?'

'My orals. I'm not very strong on oral exams.'

'You speak perfectly well, Kelsey.'

'Not in exams. I want to practise. When can I see you?'

Esmerelda was a little surprised. No one in the seg unit had ever asked her for extra help. Men on the open wings asked for extra help all the time, but they didn't down here. She was accustomed to coming into the closed unit and then being able to leave.

'Can you come tomorrow?' Kelsey could see Esmerelda hesitating. 'Please?'

Esmerelda consulted her diary. 'I have half an hour tomorrow morning before lock-up.'

'Good,' said Kelsey. 'I'll see you then.'

The next morning while Esmerelda was getting ready to go to work, she went into the bathroom to pick up her lipstick. She put some on, and put the tube into her purse. In the mirror, her make-up looked fine, she was wearing enough. Still, she picked up her mascara, her eye-liner, her eyebrow pencil. She rummaged through the make-up bag she kept beside the sink. She found some eye-shadow, other shades of lipstick, an old pair of fake eyelashes. She picked up the entire bag and put it in her briefcase.

Esmerelda got down to the seg unit a little early; Kelsey was waiting for her. They walked past the cells on the way to the interview room, where it's a bit more quiet, Kelsey said. They embarked on a practice exam; Esmerelda opened her case to find her notes. She brought out the make-up bag instead.

Cleanser, moisturiser, foundation, toner, powder, blush: Kelsey looked best with a dark brown eye-liner, black mascara, his eyebrows darkened and made thick. Esmerelda found it easy to touch him. He tilted his face back and let himself be touched. They consulted the mirror in her compact. Kelsey knew more about make-up than Esmerelda; this did not surprise either of them. 'But your skin . . .' said Esmerelda.

'I know. It's all the drugs I've been taking. For the change – as though I'm bloody menopausal already,' he laughed. 'My skin's gone all funny. But apparently it will clear up again.'

'What's going to happen?' asked Esmerelda.

'Well, I suppose I'll have to be moved to a women's prison sometime soon. Maybe after the surgery.'

Esmerelda held her breath.

Kelsey smiled and said, 'That will be weird. In all of London I'll bet I'm the only girl in a men's prison.'

'You're not a girl yet,' said Esmerelda.

'Well,' said Kelsey, 'nearly.'

A SPECTACULAR VIEW

The sun was shining. This was not unusual. It glinted on the distant peaks with their tiny, almost-melted snow caps. Linda breathed in huge great gulps of crystalline air. She leaned over the parapet, scraping back her hair, tilting her birdy-featured face towards the sky. The sun glared down at her. Her skin felt hot, especially around her eyes. The thick glass of her spectacles refracted and redistributed the rays. Would her glasses act like magnifying lenses, she wondered? If she stood like this for long enough would her face eventually catch fire?

Bob tugged at her shorts like a child.

'Don't do that, Bob,' Linda murmured. 'You'll pull them off.'

Bob growled and said, 'Mmm.'

'Not here,' Linda said. She continued to point her face towards the sky, eyes closed. She listened to Bob's footsteps on the gravel as he wandered away.

Linda spread her arms and stretched in the heat. She felt wonderful, well-fed, well-holidayed. Granada was a fine place, a lovely place, she thought, the Alhambra magnificent. She opened her eyes a fraction, squinting. It was awful not being able to wear dark glasses. Linda could not see without her ordinary glasses, but purchasing prescription sunglasses seemed too vain and she had

87

never been able to bring herself to wear clip-ons. They reminded her of her father who used to come home drunk from the golf club, his clip-ons askew, cracked and smeared with sweat. Trips into town he would wear his clip-ons flipped up, Linda cringing at his side, hoping they wouldn't run into anyone she knew.

Bob did not wear glasses. He was one of the Olympians, blessed with 20/20 sight. Linda hoped their unborn children would be like Bob in that way, their clean and pretty faces free of impediment.

Still, Bob usually had his face hidden behind something when they were on holiday, binoculars, cameras, video equipment. Linda did not mind; she liked her husband to have hobbies, it filled up his spare time. Anything was better than golf.

In her own spare time Linda made jewellery. She had discovered this vocation at age seven when she broke her first pair of glasses. They snapped at the nose piece when Linda was hit in the face with a flying gym shoe one day at school. Once she recovered her equilibrium she broke off the arms, stuck gold stars onto the lenses and wore them on a string around her neck. Since then she had collected old spectacles, monocles, bifocals, trifocals, sunglasses (no clip-ons), pince-nez, and reading glasses as well as lenses from microscopes, viewfinders, periscopes, telescopes, and, with Bob's help, all manner of camera lens – tinted, zoom, wide-angle, fish-eye. She would spend hours transforming these bits into glittering, rather avant-garde accessories, the kind of jewellery that dazzled babies. Her favourite piece was her own wedding ring which she had made out of an old pair of her mother's hard contact lenses. It reflected light as well as any diamond and had saved Bob a great wodge of money.

Linda opened her eyes wide and leaned over the parapet. A line of perspiration formed across her brow and began to trickle down between her eyebrows. She stretched her arms out over Granada. White buildings climbed the hill opposite. Linda leaned further out, daring herself. She looked around to make sure no one was watching. She pulled off her headband and shook her head. Her hair felt soft and clean. She leaned right over the warm stone wall, her hair feathering around her face. She took a deep breath. Then her foot slipped on the gravel and she jerked back to stop herself from falling. As she moved, her glasses slipped off her face. She felt the arms ease out from behind her ears. She gasped – there was nothing she could do. Her spectacles plummeted to their death one hundred–plus feet below.

Where was Bob?

Linda sat on the parapet. She looked down. Even her knees were a bit blurry now. Everything had become indistinct, the world was suddenly muffled and distant. She really could not see. There she was, blinded and alone on top of an ancient monument like some tragic figure out of Homer or Shakespeare.

She tried to slow down her breathing and began to rock back and forth, mumbling to calm herself. 'This is my worst nightmare,' she began. 'This is what I dream about when I am feeling particularly anxious. It's why my mother always told me to carry an extra pair of glasses while travelling. Of course, I don't, I've never done what she tells me to do. "Boys don't make passes at girls who wear glasses" as my Aunt Betty once told me. And they don't, it's true, except Bob and he's sort of blind in a friendly, dog-like kind of way. And sport, I could never play sport properly, I always thought my glasses would fall off. Can't swim because I can't see, have never been able to see my feet in the shower, never know if I'm clean or not, vulnerable at night, and every morning for how many years? I've had to search my entire bedside table in the hope of eventually locating where I deposited the stupid things the night before. The world is cruel to spectacle-wearers. People automatically assume I'm more intelligent than I actually am. It would have been all right if I'd been a genius as well as short-sighted, but I'm not. Things never work out that way.'

Linda had always had problems buying glasses because when she tried on a new pair she could not actually see what she looked like wearing them. These days she took Bob with her to the opticians although he had not proved all that useful. 'You look fine love,' was his usual comment although once or twice he said 'No, those are not for you,' rather firmly. Still, it was important to Linda to have Bob's approval; she could go through her day thinking, well, at least Bob loves me.

Linda looked up, trying to remember which part of the Alhambra she was in. She had her passport and her air ticket in her bag with her and the phrase book she and Bob had bought in case they had to speak Spanish for some unforeseen reason, not that it would be of any use to her now. She could just sit there and wait for Bob to come back. That's what she would do. He would remember he had a wife eventually, wouldn't he?

Linda remembered when she and Bob first met. It had been at a party given by a mutual friend. Bob stumbled up to her around midnight. He had been drinking and his speech was a bit slurred. 'I bet,' he said slowly, 'when you take off those glasses you are actually quite good-looking.'

Linda was shocked. 'I don't,' she replied.

'Don't what?'

'Take them off.' She and Bob danced, retiring to a dark corner quite quickly. Linda had been drinking as well. They were both rather younger then.

They'd been seeing each other for a couple of weeks before Linda actually let Bob take off her glasses. 'Oh,' he said, 'you look just the same.'

'Disappointed?' she asked.

'No,' he replied. They were married within six months.

Linda tried to look around, to see what she could see. The Moorish splendour of the Alhambra had disappeared. Might as well be in Swindon, she thought. Dotted here and there were what she took to be other tourists in brightly coloured clothes, a smudge of yellow, a drop of red, a scream of lime-green. Where had Bob gone? In the background, all around, was the orange dirt, clay and brick of the buildings, silver-green olive trees, lemon trees with dots of yellow, purple and red bougainvillea, all smeared across the blue sky, like in a modern painting. Linda could see the colours, that was not a problem. It was the shapes that were indistinct, the shapes that lay beneath the colours. If in the space of time between when her glasses had plunged to their destruction and this moment now Granada had been taken over by brightly dressed aliens Linda would have been none the wiser. With this thought she looked back down at her knees.

Hanging from her neck was a piece of her own jewellery, a pendant made of a monocle encrusted with seashells and sequins. She lifted it towards one eye and looked through. It was like trying to see through spectacles made from the bottoms of coke bottles.

Why didn't someone speak to her? Couldn't they tell she needed help? Wasn't there some other English tourists nearby? What had Bob been wearing? Bob, she thought fondly, my husband. What did Bob look like, in fact? Perhaps with the glasses her memory had gone as well. Linda could picture his face, still, like a photograph, but she realized that was how he had looked when they met. Hadn't he aged since then? Was his nose really that straight, his eyes that clear?

Linda felt alarmed. What did Bob look like? She could visualize him — sort of — his face behind a camera, his body crouched behind a tripod. He was hers, they belonged together, they were married. Where was he when she needed him, needed to be reminded of him?

Anything could happen to her now, Linda thought, anyone could come over to her and claim to be Bob and if he sounded like Bob, felt like Bob, she'd be his. She thought about her alien theory again. Or worse, what if war had been declared suddenly. Perhaps Spain had just invaded Gibraltar? Linda had always known that during wartime the first thing that would happen would be she'd lose her glasses. They would be snatched off her face by some marauding soldier, blown away by explosion or fire. Buffeted about by whatever came her way, led around by benevolent strangers, she would end up in a prison camp for people who have lost their glasses.

Linda stood. She had to do something, she couldn't just sit there and wait forever. She had to find Bob or, at least, someone who could help her find Bob. Taking one cautious step forward, she swayed. She felt heavy and immobile, as though she was made from old stone like the Alhambra itself. With her specs she had lost her sense of balance as well as her memory.

She could not see where she was going. The sun felt very hot. Linda moved towards some yellow and green blobs – Italians – then over towards some red and black – Japanese. She felt dizzy, and her knees buckled. She sat down in the dirt.

A shape rushed over. Up close, Linda could tell it was a man. He was wearing white and smelt a bit like Bob, same aftershave. He was speaking to her, in what language? 'I've lost my glasses,' Linda said. 'It's my husband, you see, I've forgotten what he looks like.' The man answered in another language, his tone reassuring. He helped her back to the parapet where she had been sitting before. He dusted her knees off and went away.

Alone again, Linda wondered how long it had been since she had last studied Bob's face, passed her eyes over his cheek. Is this what happens to all married couples – they become unable to see each other's faces? Could she remember what other people looked like, her mother, her sister, herself in fact? If she really had to, if her life depended on it (like it almost did now), would she be able to describe the people she loved most? Would she be able to recall what made their faces different from all the others?

The sun was getting hotter. Linda shielded her eyes and squinted and looked around again. Was that Bob shimmering through the air up ahead? The shape turned and wobbled through the heat haze towards her. If Bob ever found her again – she put her chances at 50/50 – and took her back to the hotel, back to England, Linda would get a new pair of glasses. She would keep them spotless and tend their hinges and buy one of those strings that lead from one arm to the other around the back of the head. She would look at her life very closely. She would memorize all the corners and ways of Bob's face so that if she ever did lose her glasses once and for all there would be at least one thing she could still clearly see.

FORCIBLY
BEWITCHED

Lois stood behind a woman whose grey-blonde hair
was cut in a perfect line across her neck, like a
bleached Louise Brooks. They were both attempting to look at a painting on the wall, but were stuck
behind a woman pushing an elderly man in a wheelchair.
The family resemblance between the pusher and the
pushed was remarkable; Lois had noticed the pair earlier
when someone else behind whom she had been standing
whispered, 'Isn't that Sir Harold Arnold?' The gallery
was very crowded. In a moment the wheelchair would
roll on to the next painting, the blonde Louise Brooks (it
was dyed, it had to be – now that Lois had started dyeing
her hair she took pleasure in assuming that everyone else
did too) would have a look and then Lois could take her
turn to gaze at the painting, at the two-hundred-year-old
blobs of oil and egg-wash or whatever it was that painters
used to fix the canvas back then.

There was a man following Lois, she was almost sure
of it, although he might be following Louise Brooks; in
fact, come to think of it, Lois was following Louise,
everybody was following everybody else around the
concourse of the gallery. Lois looked forward to the day
she could view the paintings on CD-Rom internet

E-Mail and would no longer have to visit museums and galleries in person. But then, she liked the crush of popular shows. Her mother had always seen picture-viewing as a chance for 'a bit of a stroll'; she was an eternal dieter and relished the opportunity to do two things at once: culture and exercise, hence a brisk walk around a large museum before tea and cakes. Lois saw the insides of a lot of museums when she was a child, but she had never been allowed to linger over the antiquities, so now when she went to exhibitions she proceeded very slowly and sat a lot, gazing at the paintings, stepping up close to peer at the brush work. Francisco Goya painted that with his own hands, she found herself thinking today, he himself stepped up to the easel on his short legs and applied his brush to the canvas. Painting seemed a physical art; Lois wished she was an artist instead of working in an office, but she knew that was like wishing she had been an astronaut.

Sir Harold Arnold's daughter pushed her father's wheelchair onward and Louise Brooks shuffled ahead and Lois took a step too, then stopped, and the person behind trod on the back of her heel. Lois hated when that happened. She turned to see who had done it. It was him, the man who had been following her. He was short, he had longish, curly black hair, and he smiled up at her rather uncertainly after murmuring an apology. 'Let's get out of here,' he said, taking a step backward into the middle of the room, the space suddenly, miraculously, clear. He reached out and took her hand and took another step backward, drawing her with him, and for a moment Lois thought he was going to burst into song. She held her breath. Was this how it felt to be in a musical? She waited.

But he did not sing. He dropped Lois' hand and said, 'Only joking.' Lois frowned and turned to discover she had lost her place in the crowd snaking round the walls of the gallery. She turned back to admonish Mr Friendly but, of course, he was gone.

Lois managed to insert her body into a gap in the queue and she viewed the rest of the exhibition happily. She had slipped away from the office early; if her boss mentioned it tomorrow she had only to tell him where she had been and, impressed by her edification, he would not mention it again. He was like her father that way, easily over-awed by culture, ashamed of his own ignorance. Lois' father had never accompanied his wife and daughter on their jogs around museums; just as well, thought Lois now, gives me something to do if he winds up in a wheelchair.

Lois had married at twenty-two, divorced at twenty-eight, and now, at thirty-two, found herself ensconced in a dwarfish spinsterhood which she rather enjoyed. She had a nice flat, a good job, friends, and she lived near Sainsbury's. Movies, books, a little theatre, restaurants, shopping, cooking, the odd holiday – a lot of flavour, but no spice, as her mother was fond of saying. Lois did not care what her mother thought, and her mother knew it, the disapproved of marriage, then the unheard of, unmentionable, divorce had ensured that. Lois liked the way her life had turned out; being on her own had not made her unhappy. However, she was not altogether sanguine about the lack of spice.

When Lois emerged blinking from the gallery into the summer haze of pollen and pollution, her man sat waiting in the forecourt of the gallery. His little legs were crossed and he grasped one knee with both hands as he watched Lois come down the steps towards him. His hair seemed even curlier in the humidity. Lois sat beside him.

'I thought you were going to sing in there,' she said.

'So did I, but it seemed inappropriate somehow,' he replied.

Lois found herself agreeing to go have coffee and, as they walked in companionable silence – it was too hot to speak – she found herself thinking that she had never done this before, accepted an invitation from a complete stranger. But then she corrected herself – I can be so deluded sometimes – because the truth was she did this kind of thing all the time.

There had been that man she met on a bus, she had gone for a drink with him; his eyes were so blue. He was Polish and once he had told her that he might as well have given up there and then because Lois could not stop thinking about the word Polish and was it really spelt just like polish and how unfortunate. Then there had been that Nigerian man who had turned out to be very rich; Lois had gone out to dinner with him, but they had disagreed about politics. Lois could be shockingly left-wing – she shocked herself sometimes – and he had turned out to be amazingly right-wing. She let him pay for dinner. And there had been that man she met in a bookshop when they both reached for the only copy of *Pride and Prejudice*. But she had married him: never trust a man who reads Jane Austen was the lesson she learned from that. One of the lessons.

'Do you read Austen?' she asked the short man who walked beside her now.

'Auster?' he asked, but just then they came to a busy road; their destination was on the opposite side. He took her by the hand once again. His hand was smaller than hers, cool and dry, which was commendable given the heat. I like a man with cool, dry hands, she thought, and then they made their dash, his five-foot-six frame sure-footed next to her five foot ten.

Lois' mother had a thing about men and height; the only good men were tall. Lois' father was six foot seven, which even now seemed a little extreme. When Lois was young she had fallen for her mother's height fetish and the man she married was a decent six foot three. But it turned out to be a disastrous misconception, one of many of which her mother was fond, like only married women can use tampons and only widowed women wear black. Life was just not like that any more.

The coffee house was busy but they found a table near the back. 'Did you see the painting?' he asked.

'Which one?'

' "Forcibly Bewitched".'

Lois recalled it; a priest with mad, rolling eyes was lighting an oil lamp held by the devil, a grey, horned satyr, while donkeys danced upright on their hind feet in the background. It was one of a group of paintings of flying witches, cannibals, and lunatic asylums, the kind of thing for which she appreciated Goya.

'Yes, I saw it.'

He nodded, he seemed satisfied.

'You are an incredible beauty,' he said.

Now this was something new to Lois. No strange man with whom she had gone off had ever said anything like that to her before. She nodded, but did not reply. What did he mean by 'incredible'? Did he mean strange? Did he mean surprising, as in not to be believed, as in weird? Did using the words incredible and beauty together actually cancel them both out leaving only ugliness in their stead?

Lois thought about this while she looked at her short, curly-haired companion.

'I meant incomparable,' he said.

'Oh,' replied Lois, 'well, that's all right then.'

Their courtship took place quickly. Lois found herself entirely enamoured. His name was Beverley and she was enchanted by the idea of having a boyfriend with a girl's name, as if that might mean he would have fewer of the foibles of previous lovers, more of the charms of a good friend. She loved to tower over him in public and he seemed to enjoy it as well; it became a kind of secret joke between them, creating a *frisson* Lois imagined somehow akin to S&M. It felt kinky. She was excited by it.

They began spending all their free time together. They went to every exhibition in the city that summer, the more crowded the better. Bev would follow directly behind Lois and, in the crush of beholding great art, Lois would feel Bev's body pressed to hers, her buttocks level with his abdomen. She would find herself blushing and, when there was room, she would turn to face him and he would smile at her silkily. Once, just once, he actually did sing. It was an aria from an opera they had recently attended; the lover dies and as she dies, she sings. Bev kept his voice low, he held both of Lois' hands, she caught and held his words even though they were Italian. None of the other exhibition-goers seemed to notice what was happening. It was as though Beverley and Lois were in a higher place.

AN ORGANIZED
RELIGION

Trains continued to shunt up and down the country despite the fact that scarcely no one could afford to ride them. Departing from King's Cross Station at 1000, 1030, 1100, on and on, over and over, the trains pulled north, into those great cathedral-stations, York, Newcastle and, finally, Edinburgh, blowing black smoke up into the arches.

Jenny travelled by train because somebody else paid for it. When asked what she did she would always reply, 'I'm in business.' 'Business' had become one of those words people use to explain a complex range of activity from multinational-backward-buyout-take-over-bids to selling drugs on the street, a word that made people nod their heads sagely when they heard it, asking no further questions. A that-explains-it-all word, like 'illness'. Taking care of business. Easier than explaining to people that she was an accountant, crunching numbers on her computer all day long. Her long-term project was the total realignment of the company's accounting process. Jenny enjoyed her work.

Jenny worked for an English company that specialized in manufacturing goods with a Scottish theme. Scotprod had recently had tremendous success with a line of ready-to-wear kilts made from a blue and green tartan which incorporated a tiny block print of a haggis. Jenny thought the haggis looked more like bagpipes, but without the pipes, just a dangly grey bag. No one else seemed to notice. These products were very popular with tourists who visited Scotland to find their roots.

The trains were remarkably punctual. Jenny nearly always got to her Edinburgh meetings on time. She would arrive lugging her big bag full of papers – one shoulder pulled down by the weight, the other forced upwards – to sit amidst the men with their dark suits and slim attaché cases. The men would ask each other's opinion about this or that, get the only other woman present, the secretary, to make coffee, show charts, give demonstrations, and arrange to meet for drinks later, sometimes including Jenny, sometimes not. But Jenny was there and this, she thought, was a victory. This was modernity. She was good at numbers, numbers were her thing. A woman in a man's world. This was business.

Then one day one of the men took Jenny aside and whispered in her ear that it had been decided she was no longer needed at these meetings. In fact, the company no longer needed her at all. 'I expect you'll be glad to hear it, my dear. You must be tired of that endless journey. Those horrible sandwiches. You'll be glad to spend more time at home, I should think. You could have a baby or something nice like that.'

Jenny did not know what to say. 'But, my project,' she stuttered as he turned to walk away, the creases in his trousers bunching up behind his knees. 'My project, it's not finished.'

'Your project?' he said, pausing to give her an avuncular

smile. 'This is the world of business, love, not infant school.'

That afternoon, as Jenny stood in the station waiting for the train, she noticed the glass in the roof overhead was broken. Rain dripped slowly down onto the platform; the water looked black and thick, it left a stain on the ironwork as well as the concrete below. The train was on time and empty as usual and Jenny sat next to the window. She took her papers, her laptop computer, her mobile telephone and her portable printer out of her bag and spread the technology across the table so that no lonely fellow travellers would be tempted to join her. Then she opened the novel that she was reading and tried to stop herself from feeling too upset.

Jenny's rise in the world of business has been sudden, like an unexpected fountain in a still pond. She had left teaching depressed by the stream of children, endlessly arriving, making a lot of noise, and then inevitably flowing away, like standing under Niagara Falls, she thought. Business had seemed the only way to go – it was either that or lose the house – and she'd always been good at numbers. She and her mother – they lived together, Jenny had been married twice but she always came home in the end – had been poor before and neither wanted to repeat the experience. Now what would she do? The novel wasn't gripping enough to stop her from panicking. And she had forgotten to get her mother one of those kilts.

As the train cut through the suburbs, past the massive old buildings overhanging the Tyne and into the shelter of Newcastle Station itself, Jenny noticed a group of young men standing on the platform. There were ten or twelve of them, all wearing scruffy anoraks, their woolly hats pulled down low over their brows, sandwiches stuffed in pockets, Thermos flasks poking out of knapsacks. They had their notepads open and were scribbling, examining Jenny's train then glancing back down at their notes, at the front and rear of the train, and then back down again. They talked and gestured animatedly, flapping their arms, looking excited. Jenny wondered what they were doing. As her train began to depart and she saw them run to a different platform she realized they were trainspotting.

Trainspotting. What an incredibly useful thing to do, Jenny thought. Almost as useful as what she had spent the last few years doing. At least they do it together, she thought. At least they do it with friends.

Jenny played with her machines for a while but there was no one to fax any more. She could have called her mother to tell her the news, but she could not face that yet. The novel was beginning to annoy her. She went to the buffet car for tea.

Later, Jenny gazed out the dirty window at the passing scenery. Britain seemed so flat from the train, one flat green plateau from north to south. In Britain the train never had to struggle through mountain passes nor cling to cliffsides as she imagined it might in other places, South America for instance. Flat country, flat people, Jenny thought looking down at herself. 'Flat-chested,' she said, almost out loud.

As the train pulled into York, Jenny noticed that here the crowd of trainspotters was much bigger than it had been in Newcastle. There were trainspotters dotted all through the station, ten or more on each platform. She could see them in the station bar and in the newsagents, comparing notes. When the train came to rest Jenny realized they were shouting to each other, one group hailing the next. She walked down to the end of the empty carriage. She leaned out of the window and listened. Boys with high voices, teenagers with the cracking tones of adolescence, men with deep voices, fathers trying to speak with authority; the trainspotters were yodelling to each other, names of trains, a jumble of numbers, times, dates.

'1982 . . .'

'Twelve carriages . . .'

'Quarter past four . . .' Britain is so small, Jenny thought as she listened, the passage of a train is a spectator sport. Everything is a spectator sport. People watch without taking part. Still, Jenny reasoned, at least they had something to do.

The engineer was blowing his whistle so Jenny shut the window and the carriage moved smoothly away, gliding along the platform, speeding up past the men and boys and their expectant, appreciative faces. As she walked back to her seat the train shuddered gently as though with a premonition. Moments later it shuddered again, more forcefully, then wheezed to an abrupt stop, still within the station. Jenny heard a loud clang and the train gave off a sort of moan. She knew she would be in York for a while.

Pulling up her coat like a blanket, Jenny fell asleep. She dreamed of dancing haggises, chopped down in their prime by the men in suits. When she awoke the station was nearly dark, low-burning yellow lamps throwing off dim light. She yawned and stretched as she looked out the window. The platforms on both sides of the train were crowded. There were hundreds and hundreds of men and boys, more trainspotters than she had ever imagined there could be in the world, let alone York. They were overhead on the walkways. They were corralled onto the next platform. Perhaps they were even on the roof of the train itself. The window between her and them vibrated as though with the sound of drums. Jenny got up slowly. She walked through the carriage and opened the window again.

The trainspotters were calling to each other. They had given up discussing trains and moved on to other topics.

'There are so many unexplained things in the world,' she heard one shout.

'There are so many reasons why one thing happens while another doesn't – endless chains of coincidence,' an older man cried out.

'Organized religions can begin and end wars,' shouted a boy with a round face.

'What if there were no trains at all?'

'What's the difference between a Hindu and a Catholic, a Muslim and a Protestant?'

'Would anyone like me to explain the theory of supply and demand?'

'When half the country does not vote, who wins the elections?'

It was as though Jenny's stalled train had caused a crisis of confidence in these men and boys and trainspotting had dissolved into random abstract pondering. It was as though, beneath the noble glass, iron, and brickwork of the station, thousands of performing trainspotter philosophers had been created spontaneously.

'What is a Mormon?'

'If a house is not a home when no one is in it, is a chair still a chair once it's broken?'

'Why are some persecuted and others not?'

'Why are some prosecuted and others not?'

'Is this the gospel according to Robert?'

'How can taxation be fair?'

'What's the difference between a trainspotter and someone who collects records?' a man yelled. When he could pick out no answer from the cacophony of voices, he shouted – she saw his face screw up with the effort – 'MUSIC! It heals you like faith,' she could still hear his voice, 'it makes you feel human. Sometimes it's hard to believe in trains.'

Jenny thought that these last comments might be thought of as heretical but none of the other boys and men seemed to notice. She wondered what the married ones had told their wives they were going to do when they left home that evening. They probably said 'business' and left it at that.

WILLOW

She knew there was a shortage of work everywhere
but she thought her own personal shortage must be
exceptional. She was getting behind with her share
of the mortgage. Departments were slimming all over
the country; education had become anorexic. The collage
of bits of work she had glued together over the past ten
years fell apart. Women's Studies was no longer an area
of academic growth.

So when May read the small advert in the local
newspaper – 'HMP Willow Education Department seeks
Lecturer in Women's Studies for part-time foundation
course for prisoners intending to do degrees' – she rang
up about it immediately. The man on the other end of the
telephone line was friendly, a loud Scottish voice. 'Come
on over to meet us,' he said, 'I'm inviting the first ten
callers. Like winning a prize.'

The following Monday May drove out into the
countryside, wind and rain lashing the car's small metal
body along narrow roadways. She'd never been to the
prison before despite having lived in its vicinity for years.
As she pulled into the parking area, the rain stopped and
she saw cars lined up neatly, red postbox, green lawn,
flowers. Her eyes lingered on these bright things as she
approached the gates. She hadn't expected the prison car
park to be so ordinary.

When she arrived home afterwards May went into the kitchen and sat down at the table. Clare was cooking, listening to the radio. She turned around and, seeing May's face, said, 'Oh sweetie, you didn't get the job.'

'No,' replied May, 'I did.'

First class of the term. 'All right,' she cleared her throat. 'Thank you for coming.' Twelve men sat behind twelve tables. Shaved heads, tattoos, a superabundance of biceps: she convinced herself that she was not visibly shaking. As she looked at them she could not stop herself from thinking, *these men have done terrible things.* 'We haven't had much feminism in here,' Ian, head of department and owner of the Scottish voice, had said when briefing May in his office. 'This is a prison for lifers – you only get life for arson or murder. In fact, a lot of these men have killed their wives.' He laughed in his hearty, catching way. 'That's just the kind of place this is.' And she laughed too, although later she clenched her fists and practised reaching for the alarm bell in her classroom.

'All right,' she said again.

The men looked at her politely. Some were smoking tiny thin roll-ups lit with crudely fashioned lighters. She watched, spellbound, as one man flicked his flint over and over. 'We're not allowed real lighters,' he said suddenly, looking up. 'No petroleum or lighter fluid allowed. We might drink it. We might blow someone up, set them on fire.' He stretched out the wick for her to see, 'It's a string from a mop-head jammed into a bit of wood with the flint attached to that. We're allowed to buy flints.' May stared as the man tugged on the mop-string wick. 'They have trouble keeping the floors clean in here.' Everyone laughed loudly.

Summer was not quite over and it was still humid; most of the men were dressed in shorts, some wore little vests instead of shirts. The display of flesh was nearly overwhelming; May kept thinking of her friend Leo and his collection of 1950s weight-lifting magazines. She hadn't been in the midst of so much masculinity for years. The nearest thing had been nights out in mixed gay clubs where the machismo was directed elsewhere and she herself was joined at the hip with Clare.

'All right,' she started again. 'Women's Studies. Over the next term I am going to try to give you an overview of the history of modern feminism, beginning with its roots in previous centuries. I want to start by getting you to tell me what you already know.'

'The best advice,' Ian had said just before she entered the classroom, 'is to teach the class exactly like you would anywhere else.'

'Aphra Behn,' said one man, thick Birmingham accent, leaning back in his seat, his hands on his gym-enhanced thighs. 'I saw a play of hers once with my wife.' Was that before you killed her or after, May did not ask. Ian had also said that the best defence was not knowing what the men had done, not knowing the crime committed, tried and sentenced for. She wasn't good at remembering names from newspapers and she avoided reading about most crime anyway, not interested in the manhunts, in the big, sensational trials. They are like students anywhere, she told herself, their options are just a little more limited.

'Madonna,' said someone else, a Jamaican inflection in his voice, 'ain't she a feminist?'

'Women are okay,' added another, 'it's just those feminazis that I can't stand.'

May took a deep breath.

And so the class began, heading into territory strange and familiar, May's course plan leading backwards into history. Two ninety-minute sessions per week, covering as much material as they could: Mary Wollstonecraft, Jane Austen, Mary Seacole, Simone de Beauvoir. Often men were missing for one reason or another – visits, appointments with probation officers, psychologists, review boards, ill health, 'having a bit of a difficult time,' whatever that meant. She learned things about them and about the rules of prison life, little things, favourite films, favourite books, which prison officers were trusted, which were not. There was not a lot of time for chatting, and May tried to avoid gaps. She found the men intelligent, eager to learn, not at all resistant to what she had to say, though keen to argue, debate. They did not ask personal questions of her and she did not of them. When she walked through the prison gates at 8:30 in the morning, normal life – Clare, shopping trips, walks in the evening, the local swimming pool, the garden – fell away.

Dresses and skirts were out of the question, fine in class but too nerve-racking out in the prison generally where she was likely to turn a corner and come upon a large group of men she had never seen before, lurking, joking, generating that particular prison smell she took home with her class's notebooks, eau de gym, eau de kitchen. She dressed more butch than she had in years, borrowing Clare's Doc Martens, tailored trousers, jackets and shirts. There were more women working in the prison than she had thought at first, it was reassuring to find she was not a complete one-off, an oddity. But in a life spent for the most part in the company of women it seemed strange to feel so utterly and distinctly female, to be in a place where her gender was such an enormous, defining thing. To be in a place surrounded by men, men, men; on good days it struck her as absurd, and hugely entertaining, like being in a Busby Berkeley production number, or a Mae West movie, just her and the boys.

'Have you come out to them yet?' asked a friend, Susan, over dinner one evening. Behind her back she was known as 'O Earnest One'; the importance of being Ernestine.

'What?' May and Clare spoke simultaneously.

'Have you told them you're queer?'

'No, I . . .'

'They'd eat her alive,' said Clare.

'No they wouldn't . . . maybe . . . they'd . . . I don't know,' said May.

'Do you think they fantasize about you?'

'What?' Once again, May was shocked by Susan's question.

'You know, do they imagine that you're their girlfriend? Do they think about you at night?'

'I don't know. Christ. I don't care.' She hadn't thought about this, or rather, she had, but she pushed it out of her mind. She wanted it to stay out of her mind. Of course they fantasized about her, their contact with women was so limited. She herself spent a lot of time thinking about them. Not that way but, nonetheless.

Her twelve men got on well, they were accustomed to working, to studying. All of them had ended up in Women's Studies in such a circuitous manner – crime, arrest, remand, court, gaol, education, Women's Studies – that they were like the best of mature students, there for a purpose, wanting to pass. Some mornings as May stood in the classroom waiting for them to be allowed off the wings they would arrive one at a time, shy to begin with, as though they were surprised to see her there yet again, vying with each other to be the most chivalrous, the most studious. They paid attention to her, these men. But then again, May thought, they had no choice.

One day she was half an hour late, held up by security at the gate, a random bag search – the officers were especially concerned with her unopened box of tampons. She arrived, breathless, sweating, to find her men sitting patiently.

'I'm so glad you waited for me,' she said blushing.

'We're accustomed to waiting,' said Alan, the one from Birmingham. 'It's one thing we get to do a lot in here.'

Some days it was difficult to keep their attention, as though their thoughts were being pulled elsewhere. What was out there in the prison, May wondered, beyond the classroom walls, that could make them seem so distracted? May found herself reworking her course plan, trying to make the connections between their own lives and women's history more concrete, obvious. She left out certain sections: Sappho, domestic violence, Vita Sackville-West. She did a session on the history of Tupperware, labour-saving convenience and the women's sales network, the revolution in work from the home. They found this hilarious, and enjoyed it, and could see what she meant, so she gained confidence; a history of contraception and reproduction politics came next. She taught that class without embarrassment until somebody started laughing and Jim told her they would have to pay the rest of Education to stay away once word got out about their course work.

And she was tough with them, as she would have been with any class. As she relaxed, and they relaxed, she stopped letting them get away with certain comments and jokes, firing back her own. She stopped wondering what they had done, she no longer had to try to prevent herself from thinking about the crimes. She found herself wondering who they really were, and what life in HMP Willow was really like. It seemed impossible to imagine a more loveless place. She wondered if they touched each other ever, at all, she wondered what it was like, having no one to touch. None of the men seemed to be actually, actively, admittedly, gay. All those years of abstinence, or 'prison bent' – did they dream of women's bodies as she thought she would if she was ever sent away from Clare, locked up without her lover's body to hold every night? Was this something she had in common with them then, a longing for women's bodies; was this another of the privileges she had over them – not only was she a woman, but at home another woman waited for her, ready to take her, ready to hold her, ready for her touch?

Stories cirulated around the staffroom where the teachers gossiped about their students like teachers anywhere. A prisoner had fallen in love with his probation officer; she had resigned, he had been moved to Willow and they were trying to get married but the Home Office was denying permission. Another prisoner, still insisting on his innocence after more than ten years in gaol, married the journalist who was helping him to publicize his appeal. This was an unconsummated nick union, celebrated amongst the inmates by a kind of ribald envy. May felt embarrassed by the gossip, embarrassed for the men.

'I can't understand how anyone could do it,' said one teacher, 'marry these murderers.' The other staff looked at her aghast.

'That's one way to put it,' said Ian.

'Well, that's what they are at the end of the day, murderers, aren't they?' The others muttered this and that but May pursed her lips to keep from speaking, to keep from saying that she could understand what some women might see in these men. They embodied a kind of potent masculinity – criminal, violent, surviving in this all-male environment – but at the same time they were powerless, without rights, vulnerable. A prisoner would write love letters, a prisoner would think about you, only you, a prisoner would long for your visits, long for your touch with an intensity unrivalled by any free man. This might be appealing to some women, May thought. After all, you would never have to iron his shirts.

Terry, another of her students, suggested one day that May come along to the Debating Society which met during evening association once a week. The following Thursday evening she went to the chapel where the meetings took place. Two members of the local university's debating team had come in to debate 'This House Believes that Rehabilitation Doesn't Work'. May sat beside Alan from her class. She liked Alan. Despite the tattoos and the biceps, he had a nice face, a clean, wide face.

The debate and the following discussion were fierce and absorbing. At the end the chaplain served tea. Alan fetched her a cup. 'What did you think?' he asked.

'Wonderful. Is everyone always so articulate?'

'Yes – although sometimes the language degenerates a bit,' he smiled. 'Depends how many women are present.'

'Do you debate?'

'No, I like to listen. I get too caught up, angry, stop making sense. I have trouble with my temper, like, well, you know.' His teacup rattled in its saucer as though a train was passing. 'I killed my wife.'

May did not speak.

'I didn't mean to. But I did.'

Still May did not speak.

'I hit her too hard one day.' He put his cup on the floor and clasped his hands together, firmly. 'I don't really care about being in here. I'd rather be in here than out there without her. It's why I'm taking your course – to try and understand what it's like for women, what it means to . . .' he trailed off. He was looking at May. She felt sure she was not visibly shaking. 'We never get the chance to talk much in your class.'

'I'm sorry, but I – there's a lot of material to cover.'

'Oh no, don't get me wrong, it's interesting.' He smiled his open smile.

'Good,' she said.

'It's funny, isn't it,' Alan continued, 'Women's Studies with a bunch of men like us. It makes you think.'

'What about?'

'Oh you know, the weaker sex, the war between the sexes.' He gave his shoulders a shake and then smiled. 'I think you should do a session on women who kill men.' He looked at her.

'Maybe,' May replied, 'I . . .'

'Oh don't worry,' said Alan, he was laughing now, 'I'm only pulling your leg.' Some of the others joined them and the conversation went back to the debate. May felt a drop of sweat slip down her spine.

After that it was harder to cut the discussions off in class, more difficult to decide what was appropriate, what was not. The Suffragettes and their hunger strikes led to a discussion about Willow. The men began to tell her things she did not know: more than three thousand people serving life sentences in Britain, in France less than one hundred, in Italy, seventy. Actual time served getting longer and longer. Slopping out. The punishment block. The prison hospital where you get sent when suffering from mental illness. The changing political will of the Home Secretary. 'And the food – my God, it's terrible,' someone said with real outrage.

The effect of these conversations was weird; May felt herself becoming close to these men at the same time as holding something back, remaining cautious, curious about their violence, but reining in her own voyeurism. Apart from Alan she still did not actually know what any of them had done. Their crimes and, hence, they themselves, remained enigmatic, mysterious. She could never know what their lives were really like.

Increasingly May found it difficult to talk about her job. She would come home to Clare and try to speak calmly, but end up blurting out stories in an unedited stream. 'I asked Terry for his essay today. He hadn't done it. I felt so sad, he's bright, he could get a good grade. He said he was having trouble working, he couldn't see his way through. "It's doing my head in," he said, "a life sentence. I've still got no idea when I'll be eligible for parole – five, ten, twenty years. They keep changing the rules, the regulations. It's doing my head in – I can't work, can't read, can't sleep."' Terry had spoken in the few moments before the end of class and the arrival of the prison officers. '"It's like Kafka," he said, "even when you know you are guilty."' May looked at Clare as she spoke, she watched the expression on her lover's face. Clare opened her mouth and then closed it again, as though there was nothing for her to say.

'Well, you can't reform the entire prison service yourself May.'

'I know Clare,' said May, shrugging and smiling. 'But what's to be done with these guys?'

That night when she and Clare got into bed May felt tense as she approached her lover, pushing her face into Clare's neck ferociously. Clare giggled and slid her body under May's, stroking May's back. They moved together and as they did May looked down at Clare's nakedness and found herself wondering if she could kill her, if she could murder the person she loved most. In what circumstances would she do it? What would it take? How would it feel? Would Clare fight back or would she just surrender? May banished these thoughts as she fought back a surge of nausea, shocked to find it coupled with desire.

FATHERS

Carlotta and Boris were childhood sweethearts. They were introduced by their mothers in the playground when they were both three years old. Carlotta had never seen a boy like Boris before; he had red hair. Boris had never met anyone like Carlotta before; she stared at him without blinking. From that first meeting they were hooked.

They continued to meet in the playground where they would sit on the swings together. Soon their mothers stopped feeling they needed to accompany them. Other children arrived and departed, games were won and lost, bodies were scraped and wounded, but always, in the end, Carlotta and Boris were left on the swings until their mothers came to drag them away.

They grew up together like seeds planted in a garden at the same time. When they were eight they played Cowboys and Indians – they took turns invading and avenging, tying each other up. When they were ten they discovered Doctors and Nurses, ordering each other to remove those trousers please, performing exploratory surgery. Somehow these two games got confused – Cowboys and Doctors and Indians and Nurses – so that by the time they were thirteen Carlotta was insisting that Boris get undressed before she tied him up with the skipping rope, and vice versa. They alternated between victor and vanquished, they gave each other equal opportunities to be bed-ridden or bossy.

Carlotta's father, Alex, was an ugly man whose passions lay hidden by an impossibly grumpy demeanour. He seemed to hate everything and everyone, including his wife. However, somewhere, deep down, he did have a good side, a happy side, and, occasionally, he gave a glimpse of it to Carlotta. As a result, the girl was his puppet, she would do anything for him, fetching newspapers, slippers, presenting him with drawings she made at school. Alex had a secret; the attention paid him by his little girl was his favourite thing in life.

Boris's father, Ramsey, did not have secrets, hidden sides, or favourite things. He was a handsome man, good at sports. It was clear to everyone in his family that the only thing he really cared about was his job as manager of a firm of accountants. Ramsey was not an affectionate man. Yet Boris managed to garner enough love from his mother and, later, Carlotta, to keep him from psychopathology.

Boris did grow up to be a doctor, although not simply for the thrill of asking dozens of women to undress in his office. He found ill health interesting; it was exciting — titillating even — to think he might cure someone of something one day. Carlotta had wanted to be an Indian when she grew up; like most teenage girls she had particularly unrealistic dreams. From ballet dancer to great academic, Carlotta went through a stack of options all of which might have made her famous or rich. Somehow legal secretary did not have the same buzz. But it was a job, it allowed her to marry Boris before he finished medical school. They moved in together, set up a little flat where they could listen to Country & Western music. George Jones and Tammy Wynette made life seem straightforward.

Despite the twenty-year passion of their offspring, Alex and Ramsey met for the first time at the wedding. They were introduced by their wives who both felt more than a little embarrassed – embarrassed that the men had never met and, somehow, embarrassed by the men. They shook hands, sizing each other up. Neither man had expected Carlotta and Boris to take their childhood romance this far. Neither was pleased by the knowledge that having children old enough to marry meant they themselves were no longer young. Perhaps it was this that bound them together; perhaps it was something even more mysterious that made them decide to be friends.

Carlotta's father Alex was not the kind of man who had friends – he was far too grumpy and only really felt comfortable in the presence of family. Ramsey could easily be described as friendless as well – none of the men with whom he still played football every weekend would have attempted to share more than a beer in the pub after the game. These men had wives instead of friends. No one would have suspected that Alex and Ramsey could become pals.

Which was, of course, what they did become: buddies, cohorts, partners, a team. Alex started training so he could go jogging with Ramsey; Ramsey took over the accounts from Alex's firm. They spoke on the telephone often and saw each other several times each week, lunches, squash games, Saturday sport on TV. Alex joined Ramsey's football team. Both wives were annoyed by this development, and annoyed with themselves for feeling slightly suspicious, recognizing their own jealousy. The two men seemed happy, excited, as though – at last! – they were having fun. And about their fun, they were serious.

Boris and Carlotta were shocked. They had had a nice honeymoon but somehow getting married had not changed anything. Life remained the same except for this, his dad and her dad, friends. It was as though Alex and Ramsey were the newlyweds, not them.

'What do you think they see in each other?' Carlotta asked, breathlessly. She had been chasing her naked husband around the flat and had finally caught him with her lasso. She wore nothing but a pair of cowboy boots.

'Men's stuff, I guess,' Boris said, panting.

'What?'

'Oh, you know, business contacts, that kind of thing. It's like having their own miniature Masonic Lodge maybe.'

'That's sinister.'

'Rotary Club then. Kiwanis. Lions.'

'Do you think they confide in each other?'

'What is there to confide?'

'Our mothers? Their relationships? Sex?' They shivered and said 'Ugh' simultaneously.

Boris was a good doctor, Carlotta was a good legal secretary. Both worked hard and had ambitions – Boris's long hours in the hospital might one day lead to a consultancy; Carlotta was toying with the idea of becoming a lawyer. On the weekends they were exhausted, Boris had to work more often than not, Carlotta did the housework. They bought a house, a car, lots of appliances and gadgets and games, they went on holiday two or three times a year. They began to get older in an invisible way.

From time to time Boris played football for his hospital. One week they played against his father and father-in-law's team. Boris hung back for most of the game, watching the two men as they kicked the ball neatly between themselves. Ramsey, his hair standing up with wind and sweat, streaked in, took a pass from Alex and scored. Boris watched while they embraced and were patted on the backside by the rest of the lads. Ramsey raised a fist in his son's direction. Boris thought him transformed, unrecognizable. His team had been confident they would beat the old guys but, in the end, they lost.

Sometimes Carlotta went shopping with her friends on Saturday; she stockpiled cowboy boots, Western-style shirts, bolo ties, stiff blue jeans. That weekend she came home with a pair of black leather chaps. 'I'm sure,' said Boris disdainfully from his position on the couch, 'I'm sure that cowboys do not wear designer chaps for which they've paid hundreds of pounds in some ladies' boutique. In fact, I'll wager that not even cowgirls do that.'

'I can't help it, Boris,' Carlotta replied. 'I just can't help myself.' Carlotta knew that Boris would change his mind when it came time for him to undo all those buckles so he could get next to her skin. He had bought her spurs for her last birthday; they knew their way into each other's fantasies. They had been together for so long they were practically the same person; they had interfaced with each other's mainframes.

Still, they alternated parents' houses for Sunday lunch. Carlotta saw enough of her father's good side to continue to be devoted. When they were alone together doing the washing-up she tried to charm her father into telling her what he saw in her father-in-law. 'Daddy,' she said, 'how's Ramsey?'

'Oh as right as rain as ever.'

'Do you see much of him these days?'

'Same amount as always.'

'Is he . . . is he, you know, happy?'

'Happy?' Alex lowered his hands into the water. 'Lovey, what are you talking about? Do you kids need a loan or something?'

Carlotta and Boris's mothers were equally curious about what their husbands saw in each other. Jane and Shelagh did not meet often but exchanged information over the telephone. They had tried being friends over the years; it seemed logical alongside the intense relationship of the children. But Jane did not like Shelagh and Ramsey very much – she found Ramsey's coldness intimidating and thought Shelagh a bit of a snob. Shelagh had tried introducing Jane to her bridge club, but she never really fit in. This had not worried the women although at times, especially leading up to the wedding, they both thought it inconvenient they were not closer.

These spells of slight regret happened with greater frequency now that Alex and Ramsey had become such a duo. Double dates were not on the agenda. In fact it was Carlotta who first brought up the possibility. 'Why don't you and Ramsey ever take Mummy and Shelagh along when you go out?' she asked her father one Sunday.

'Mummy and Shelagh? They don't play squash, you know that,' Alex replied. 'Nor football for that matter.'

'You can't always be playing sport, you see each other too often for that.'

'We never do anything that the girls would enjoy.'

'You just like getting away from them.'

Alex huffed. If Carlotta had been nearer, and smaller, he would have cuffed her across the ear like a dog.

Boris broached the subject with his mother one day. 'Oh,' Shelagh said, as if it had never occurred to her before, 'they wouldn't go for that.'

'Why not?'

'Well . . . they have things to discuss. Neither of them are what you could call sociable. I imagine it takes all their concentration just to talk to each other. Your father would not be able to cope with a four-way conversation. And besides, I don't think he likes Jane very much.' She blushed slightly as she said this; she had no idea what Ramsey thought of Jane, they had never discussed her.

'It's not that Carlotta and I think you should all go away on holidays together or anything like that. In fact we don't care whether or not you four get along. We're the important ones.'

His mother frowned.

'It just seems a bit weird, this friendshp thing, it's gone on for such a long time. We want to know what it's about.'

'Sweetheart, you make it sound as though you wish I would spy on them.'

'Oh,' he said, 'that's a good idea.'

Shelagh blushed again. She could not say that this thought had never occurred to her.

But spying was not necessary. Ramsey came home from work on Friday night and, before opening the drinks cabinet as was his habit, handed Shelagh an envelope. Inside was a pair of theatre tickets for the following night, not a musical or anything like that, but Shakespeare. 'Dear?'

'I thought we could do with an outing,' he said, pouring her gin.

The next day when Shelagh realized Ramsey had taken his best suit out of the wardrobe she decided to get dressed up as well. He had cleaned the car that afternoon, he dropped her off in front of the theatre before parking. Shelagh glanced around furtively for Alex and Jane but there was no sign of them.

Alex and Jane were having dinner in the best restaurant in town. Candles, wine, linen tablecloth. Alex was ebullient over his asparagus, complaining about work, complaining about all manner of things. He was hardy and grouchy and Jane suddenly remembered why she had married him.

One month later, it happened again. Then the next month, and three weeks after that. Restaurants and theatres, sometimes both. 'They are having Another Saturday Night,' Carlotta would say to Boris after speaking to her mother on the telephone. It was as though their fathers had made a policy decision re: The Wives. Take them out, keep them happy. Carlotta found their behaviour almost indecent. It made Boris feel inadequate. They both felt outdone, out-romanticked as they sat in front of another lousy video, too tired from work to go out anywhere.

'Maybe Alex and Ramsey went to see a movie together or something, maybe they read the same novel and in it the male lead fell in love with his wife again and decided to start all over,' Carlotta speculated.

'They both had affairs is more like it, and then realized the error of their ways and are now making up for their sins.' Carlotta and Boris frowned. This seemed particularly distasteful.

'Or maybe,' said Carlotta before she had time to think, 'they had an affair with each other – they are having an affair with each other – and this is their way of disguising it.'

'Oh Carlotta,' replied Boris, appalled.

'Maybe not,' said Carlotta quietly.

The next Friday night Boris and Carlotta pulled themselves together and decided to go out. They put on their gear and drove to a Country & Western bar on the outskirts of town. At a gingham-covered table they sat trying to keep awake, drooping over their drinks while a local band played. In the middle of a rather good rendition of 'It Ain't Me You Love, It's Your Sister', Boris took his elbows off the table and stretched. That was when he spotted Ramsey and Alex. They were sitting at a table on the far side of the dance floor. They were both wearing Stetsons.

CELIA AND
THE BICYCLE

Celia rode a bicycle. She was too impatient to use the public transport system, in too much of a hurry with no time. For her, the bicycle was a symbol of freedom from constraint. It enabled her to overcome traffic jams, avoid potential attackers, keep in trim, and get from A to B quickly. Two wheels and a set of handlebars meant, to Celia, liberation.

Celia also wore short skirts. During the sixties when short was chic, her mother, an accomplished seamstress, had sewn a series of little red, yellow and paisley skirts for Celia. The ripped-up and anarchic fashions of punk had enabled her to continue wearing the mini while a teenager, then the eclecticism of style in the 1980s allowed her to keep her knees bare until the mini-skirt made its re-entry onto the pages of *Vogue*. But Celia was not concerned with being fashionable; she loved the mini-skirt and that was all there was to it.

For Celia, the mini-skirt was a symbol of freedom from constraint. It enabled her to pedal her bicycle without impediment. With her strong legs free from complicated trousers or the volumes of material involved in other skirts or dresses she could speed her way through the city. The tight-fitting mini-skirt made her feel powerful, spare, economical and streamlined. She thought that if her bicycle had been human it would have worn mini-skirts as well.

Unfortunately for Celia, however, the combination of bicycle and mini-skirt produced explosive reactions on the streets of the inner city. Every time she pedalled down the road she was harangued. Men, always men or does that go without saying?, were compelled to pass comment as she sailed by. 'Oi, sit on my face, sweetheart,' was a popular phrase down the Old Kent Road. 'Nice pair of legs,' was particularly common in the West End and it was not unusual for men in Camden Town to offer the wisdom of 'Don't you think your skirt is a bit short?' as if they were moral arbiters, each one. Engines were revved, windows were hurriedly rolled down, construction workers looked up from their toil.

All Celia wanted from life was short skirts, speed, and freedom. She tried to imagine ways she could get these things. If the man on the scaffolding leaned too far to the right whilst attempting to get her attention he might fall from above into the path of an oncoming car, the driver of which would also be trying to catch Celia's eye, or rather, some other part of her body. That car might swerve to miss the construction worker who by now lay crumpled on the road, running over his legs and then crashing into another oncoming car, the driver of which would also be trying to see up Celia's skirt to where the tops of her thighs meet the bicycle seat.

Celia was not a vindictive woman. She simply had a good sense of fun. She also wanted justice. She believed in justice.

Like her spirit, mind, and body, Celia's bicycle was fast and adept but fragile and vulnerable as well. Hers was not a particularly good bicycle – fairly old, both tyres were usually slightly soft and one of the lights was broken. Celia was not a Bicycle Snob. In recent years this terrifying group of people dressed in Italian cycling gear had made riding a bicycle a trendy and fashionable activity. Pushing their lean frames against the wind, the Bicycle Snobs tore up and down the streets of London, dodging traffic lights and dashing up one-way streets the wrong way. They carried complicated and expensive mechanisms for securing the dismantled frames of their well-oiled and pampered machines to lampposts and wrought-iron fences. There were also the Bicycle Couriers to contend with, people who delivered messages throughout London. Recalcitrant daredevils, driven by a mysterious death-wish, the Couriers were also Bicycle Snobs at heart. They overtook Celia on the thoroughfares and by-ways, looking down at her inferior bike with distaste. Unlike the men in cars they did not pass verbal comment, but Celia could tell what they were thinking. She did not care. Celia was a bicycle libertarian; she believed everyone should be allowed to do it their own way. To her the bicycle was a modern icon, symbolic of religious rightness and purity. Cheap, pollution-free, silent: for her it was enough simply to ride. And riding in London was an act of faith.

Celia had a recurrent dream. In this dream, which she usually had after cycling home drunk, she and her bicycle could fly. All they needed was a slight hill, like the one down Pentonville Road from the Angel to King's Cross, or the one that slides around Brockwell Park en route from Herne Hill to Brixton. Late at night with no cars around she would travel down the hill as quickly as her bicycle could take her and just before reaching the bottom, take off. Pedalling at a leisurely pace, Celia and her bicycle would glide over London like Peter Pan and Wendy, like the Wicked Witch of the West. The city sparkled in the night as they flew over the enormous rail stations and circled around Nelson's Column. Celia dreamed she had seen Nelson's face, a vision of pride covered with pigeon shit.

Upon waking the morning after having had a flying bicycle dream, Celia always felt disappointed and flat. Rubbing her eyes on the way to the bathroom she would stop in the corridor and examine her bicycle. It did not look like it could fly. After breakfast she would take it outside the front door, get on it and set off down the road. The first hill was always a terrible strain and she would huff and puff and curse. But later, as she wove between cars, passing through traffic jams with ease, she would remember her dream and take her hands off the handlebars and flap her arms like they were wings. It was the nearest she could get to the real thing.

The traffic in London creates a special form of madness that makes the ordinarily sweet-natured person aggressive and violent. Car, motorcycle, and lorry drivers become psychopaths while only bus drivers seem able to maintain calm. Cyclists are not exempt from this madness; the more lyrical and graceful movement of a bicycle does not necessarily mean its rider is not angry, does not want to kill or maim. Celia herself valued the rush of adrenalin she received when she shouted at cars that cut in front of her. 'Wrap those legs around me, love' would send her off a bit faster at the next green light. 'We've seen your legs, now show us your tits,' gave her an edge on the cyclist behind. And, 'Lucky bicycle seat,' or 'I wish my face was your bicycle seat,' or 'Is that a bicycle seat or are you excited?' would send her shooting up the next hill as though her legs were pistons and her heart a generator. She would yell back 'Fuck off' or 'Asshole' or 'Bastard' and ride like the wind. Pumping her legs up and down, up and down, she felt purified and hardened and sleek. She felt they could not stop her, they could not put reins on her, they could not suppress her energy with their remarks. She ate up their abuse like a horse eats oats and used it to fuel her journey.

One weekend Celia rose early. She was going to visit a friend who was organizing a boatload of bicycles to take to Nicaragua. Apparently in Nicaragua there was a shortage of that kind of thing. Celia opened her closet and surveyed her collection of mini-skirts. To her they looked functional and practical, like gym shorts only not quite so utilitarian. She chose a blue and white stripy one, not too short, not micro-mini, but a mini nonetheless. With that, a shirt and her plimsolls, she was ready. She ate breakfast then got on her bike.

The traffic was heavy with Saturday shopping confusion. Celia was running a bit late. At a set of traffic lights on Clapham High Street one of the stream-lined neo-Italians passed her in a flash of perfectly attired bright light. Toiling against the wind along Clapham Common, she hummed a tune and ignored the comments which were hurled at her every minute or two. She picked up a lot of speed as she reached Clapham South tube station and it was there, just beyond the intersection, that the man in the yellow Cortina chose to ignore her, swung his steering wheel and tried to take his car into a side street, whamming his foot on the accelerator. Celia's bicycle, her beloved and much adored, upright handlebar with a male cross-bar and battery operated lights bicycle, slid under the heavy bodies of this man and his metal-shelled vehicle. The wheels of the car crunched and twisted the bike's frame, snapping off the seat.

The bicycle was dead. Forever.

On initial impact Celia took off and flew through the air. For a minute that extended into hours she floated above the crowded and busy street. Clapham Common looked green and peaceful away from the road, traffic-free. The wind rushed around her legs and up her mini-skirt. The cars stopped honking, their engines stood idle, and the people on top of the buses stared, their mouths open, their noses pressed against the windows.

Then, with a thud, Celia landed on the roof of the yellow Cortina. The driver got out of the car. His face was bloated and red with anger. 'Get off my car, you fucking slag,' he shouted.

Celia felt shocked. She had just been in the air, she had actually flown and it was not a dream. 'What do you mean, you wanker,' she said. 'I'm not a slag. Don't you call me a slag. It's drivers like you who *kill* cyclists.'

'Who the fuck do you think you are, riding around London with your skirt up your arse? If you were my daughter, or my wife for that matter, you wouldn't get out the front door in that thing.'

'You almost killed me just then, you bastard.'

'Serve you right too, you little slut.'

Something inside Celia burst then. Maybe it was her inner tube or perhaps it was only a bulb in her lights, but something exploded. She stood on the roof of the yellow Cortina and shouted, 'You killed my bicycle, you animal. You're going to pay for this.' She leapt off the car and for a moment she felt free again. Then she landed on the shoulders of the driver. With her legs on either side of his head, he had become her beast of burden, her pack-horse, her mule, maybe even her bicycle. She kicked him in the ribs with her heels and reached down to slap him on the backside with one hand. 'Giddy-up, come on, let's go!' And with her powerful legs like a vice on his neck she made him carry her to the door of her friend's house, through Balham and into Tooting. On the way she decided that men were just as easy to ride as bicycles, not as quick, mind you, not as smooth, but much less work on hills.

MY MOTHER,
MY FATHER, AND ME

When I visit my father I take the train. I leave home by eleven and catch the tube, the Northern Line, to King's Cross, walk across the street to St Pancras, and take the Intercity to Market Harborough. If I get the train at noon, I arrive in Market Harborough just after one o'clock. I walk into the centre of the little town – I have got to know it quite well – and wander around. I tell myself I'm going to go into one of the pubs and have some lunch, but somehow I always feel too nervous to eat, too unsettled by the journey to sit anywhere for long. And, of course, I'm afraid that if I go into a pub everyone will look at me. Everyone will be able to tell. They will know where I am going and, in an instant, they will know who I am and what happened.

So, I avoid lingering anywhere too long, and just before two o'clock I go to a phonebox and ring for a taxi. The local firm are usually prompt, they drive up the hill out of the village in the rapid, neat manner of rural taxi-cabs. They too are accustomed to this journey.

The prison sits on top of a ridge, the highest point in the area. In winter after the sun drops away and the yellow dome lights come on, the prison glows malevolently, casting shadows over the countryside like a ghastly carved pumpkin on Hallowe'en. The ridge catches the worst of the weather, a breeze becomes a squall, drizzle becomes hard, piercing rain.

Once there, I wait with the others, all the parents, lovers, children, and friends, everyone's face taut with the same mixture of apprehension, longing, and shame. Here I have nothing to hide. In the queue for the visits room I can feel that no one will judge me, or my father.

The security procedure for the visits room, which is on the boundary of the prison, not really inside the prison itself, is complex and time-consuming, even though in recent months the authorities have made an effort to make it easier. I thought that the portakabins next to the prison gates were for the builders but it turned out — things do sometimes change between one visit and the next — that these low plywood boxes are the new visitors' facilities, the much-heralded waiting room and advice centre. At least now we can stay warm and dry while we wait.

I don't get searched all that often any more, which is the only sign that the pale-faced and nameless officers have ever seen me before. My father has been in this particular prison for several years, and I see the same officers every time I come, once a month, but they give no indication that they know me, not even the women, the female officers who have actually laid their hands on my body as they rummage through the folds of my clothes looking for contraband.

If I have brought presents for my father I hand them in to Property. I never feel certain that everything I bring will get to him, but very little has gone missing over the years. My father doesn't ask for much, magazines mostly, paperback novels the library can't get for him. I always try to bring food as well, fruit mainly, some good quality tea-bags. He insists that he can get everything he needs from the prison itself – meals, clothes, shaving gear, underwear. I once tried to replace the rubber prison slippers he wears with a pair of decent shoes. He sent the box back to me, unopened, with a letter demanding that I get my money refunded. He cannot support the idea of being a financial burden to my brother and me.

I've been coming on my own to visit for a couple of years now. Before that I always came with Auntie Ann. Auntie Ann is my legal guardian. My brother, Toby, and I lived with her after our father was sentenced. Uncle Greg lived with us as well, at first, but then they split up. Other relations worried that their divorce was hard on us, but I think by then Toby and I were immune. You could have hammered nails into our hands and we would not have felt them.

Ann is my father's sister and she has always been good to us. We didn't choose each other but, given the circumstances, everything has gone pretty well. I prefer being on my own, of course. But when you are young you can't just strike out on your own like in a children's book, you've got to be in thrall to adults for a while.

Toby used to tell other kids that we were orphans, but I've never had trouble telling people that my father is in prison. I find this information sorts out the meek from the strong.

When I was sixteen I met my first boyfriend at a party. I thought he was very fine. He asked me to dance and then we sat in a corner and talked. Turned out we went to neighbouring schools. By that time I had no trace of my old accent – Auntie Ann lived in London which was miles away from Durham, where Toby and I were born. We danced and talked and had some beer, smoked a spliff together – he was seventeen, almost eighteen. I could tell he was looking for a girlfriend and, as I was looking for a boyfriend, we got along well. We liked the same music, which is important. He liked to talk and I liked to listen to him, he liked to swear and boast and, in his way, he was charming. When I told him my father was in prison a certain look came into his eyes, a look I was familiar with. He didn't ask a single question and I guess he invented a father for me then, a bank robber most likely, maybe even a drug smuggler, or – yes – a spy. He found romance in the fact that my father was a prisoner. I didn't particularly care where it came from, any romance was enough for me.

Ann was very good at helping me buy clothes and shoes, she had a quick proficiency with make-up and hair. I don't think my own mother went in for dresses and high heels, at least not that I can remember. Sometimes when I go into department stores and walk through the cosmetics section I come across a perfume that will bring Ann to me immediately, but I have never found a scent that makes me think of my mother. I don't have any photographs of her, I don't have any of her clothes, the police confiscated everything personal and it was never returned to us. Last Christmas Toby told me he could not remember our mother at all.

Once I am allowed through to the visits room I find a table and sit down. I like to try to stay away from the large family gatherings and the young women who have come to visit their boyfriends. I find the smoking and the noise gets to me, the children always cry and end up running in and out of the room. Some afternoons the young couples will spend the whole time sprawled across the table in each other's arms and my father and I find this embarrassing. As I wait for him to arrive, I wonder how I look, hoping I appear healthy and cared for. My father and I both spend a lot of time trying not to worry each other.

Doors bang, keys and keychains clank, officers shout and eventually my father comes through the door. He keeps his prison blues very smart. He irons his prison jeans and shirts and he always wears a blue woollen prison tie for our visits. Every month I think he seems thinner, dimmer somehow, more and more faded, but this must be an illusion, he would have disappeared completely by now. He looks a tidy little old man, shrivelled and ruined.

Our visits go well, the two hours pass too quickly. I buy cups of tea from the canteen. My father drills me, and I attempt to prise information from him, what he needs, how he is coping. Sometimes when I talk to my friends about their fathers the irony catches me up and threatens to trip me – I know my father much better than they know theirs. They don't spend two hours together every month, two hours that always have and always will feel like the last two hours we may ever spend with each other. I try to bring photos or, at least, news of Toby – my brother does not visit our father himself. And my father tries to make himself understand that I am a grown woman now, that I am not a little girl, I am no longer the child witness.

That first boyfriend did not last long, first boyfriends rarely do. I was a morbid little soul and he wanted to have a good time. So did I, really, but things got in my way. I used to dream that I was in prison, that it was me alone in a cell, not my father. This dream got in our way.

My second boyfriend, a year later, was much more serious. Auntie Ann made it clear that if I was going to sleep with boys I had to take precautions, and she made this easy for me. She would not let Dorian stay the night but then, while Toby and I lived with her, she never brought her boyfriends home either. Dorian, well, Dorian was wonderful. He and I had rapport. We shared tastes and desires, our bodies rolled together like we were in the centre of a big, soft bed. When I told him about my father he did not make assumptions. He once asked if I would like him to come on a visit with me, and he understood when I explained that visits were just for my father and me. He didn't ask any more questions. Like most people, he could probably guess what had happened, and he saw it was not something I could discuss.

We went away together, stretching our student grants to trips to Amsterdam and Malaga, once as far as Morocco. After two years we decided to share a flat. Ann was very good, she made us curtains for our bedroom, drank a bottle of wine with us to celebrate the day we moved. Toby had already left – he was younger than me, but always quicker to do things – and I think Ann was not unhappy to be on her own after her years of sudden, unexpected, child-rearing.

Things began to go wrong in our third year. I had become more absorbed by my studies, I was always an earnest student, while Dorian became more and more disenchanted with his. He said he was not happy with the system, with the fact that the progress of his life seemed almost inexorable – college, work, pension, the rest of it.

He wanted fresh excitement. I felt the opposite, I expected complete disaster and so was quite happy to be confined by routine.

My father and I are very similar. I don't know if this is because of the years we spent together, or the years we've spent apart. We are both easily embarrassed – our cheeks grow ripe and red for no reason. We share moods – when I am low, so is he. We are happiest when our lives are calm and plain. We have an uneasy relationship with the world, we do not trust others lightly.

During the day I mark the time when my father's cell is unlocked. 8:00 a.m., his door is opened, he washes, has breakfast. 8:45 he is locked into the plastic injection moulding workshop where he is employed. 11:45 he picks up lunch and is locked into his cell between 12:30 and 1:45. 2:00 is back to work, 4:30 he gets his tea and is locked up again from 5:00 till 5:45. In the evening he can go down to watch television if he feels sociable. 8:00 is bang-up for the night. Twelve hours he spends alone in his cell with a bucket to piss in.

It is the night-time that I like best. After 8:00 I know where he is, I know my father is safe. I know he is listening to the radio I bought him, quiet music, or a play. Perhaps he is writing to me, or to Ann. Perhaps he is thinking about when Toby and I were small and he worked in an office and stayed home on the weekends. Maybe he falls asleep and dreams of my mother. Or perhaps my mother keeps him awake.

Dorian began to have an affair. He deceived me as though we had been married for fifteen years and had nothing left to our relationship except wedding rings, children and contempt. He was abrupt, and indiscreet as well, perhaps as indiscreet as my mother had been, I don't know. He was always late. He worried about his appearance. He whistled tunes I had never heard.

I was paralysed by his behaviour. I could not speak to, nor move away from, him. I could not confront him. I could not admit to what was taking place. I stood absolutely still, and let rage entomb me.

One night he came home about eleven o'clock. He was a little drunk. I was standing in the corridor just outside the sitting room as he came through the front door. He greeted me with happy insouciance and put his arms around me, embraced me, kissing me. I loved the feel of his body next to mine. I knew where he had been but, with his touch, I was willing to forget it.

I leaned back against the wall as we kissed. He pressed his palms against my breasts. I slipped my fingers over his belt and undid his flies and reached inside his trousers. His underwear was wet, not just damp, but wet from fucking her. I withdrew my hand sharply, but Dorian caught my wrist and pulled my hand to his groin. It was awkward, he took a step towards me, the rug slipped, we twisted around trying to stay upright and slid roughly towards the floor. I was on top of him. In fact, I had him pinned down. I sat on his legs, undid his trousers and pulled them open. He smelt very strong. I looked at him and he could see that I knew. He began to speak but stopped when I struck him across the face. Not a slap, but a punch, my knuckles stinging. I moved forward and sat on his chest, catching his arms with my legs. I hit him again, as hard as I was able. I thought if I could lift his head and knock it against the floor and . . . I looked around for something to hit him with but he was struggling against me, pounding his knees into my spine, rocking back and forth. I hung on. Then he raised his hips off the floor and threw me over onto my back, landing on top of me, forcing all the breath out of my lungs. He grabbed my hair with his hand, wrenching my head to one side, pulling my neck taut, my cheek scraping hard against the rug, my back curved unnaturally.

From where I lay I could see into the sitting room. I could see the settee where I had been watching television, and I could see myself there, twelve years old. From where I lay everything was sideways and upside-down and this is what my mother must have seen as she lay on the floor that day, my father on top of her. Her head was pulled back just like mine, her gaze wild and afraid. My father did not realize I was there but my mother saw me watching. She looked at me as I watched her die.

I don't remember my mother's character. I don't know how she ended up on that floor. If she had lived perhaps I would not be who I am. There would be more to the equation than just my father and me, our visits, our dreams, our failings. Auntie Ann tried hard, but she was only Auntie Ann. In the end, we are our parents' children.

Dorian did not hit me. He only pulled my hair to stop me from scratching him. Neither of us was very strong, but he was bigger than me. He got up and left me lying there, my head craned around, my mother, my father, and me.

It is always difficult when the visit ends. The officers start to call the time, they walk up and down between the tables rattling their chains. My father bows his head and thanks me for taking the trouble to come to visit him. I ask how much longer he thinks they'll make him serve and he says he has no idea. He doesn't want to give me false hope.

I think my father would like to die in prison. I don't know if he could survive if they let him out, if they gave him a freedom my mother will never have. But he won't die, and one day he will get out. But not now, and at the end of every visit this bears heavily on me.

A MODERN GOTHIC
MORALITY TALE

Mina lives with Vladimir in the docklands of London. Vladimir bought an enormous flat there when the area was first being redeveloped. He likes to be by the river; it reminds him of his voyaging days. The flat takes up an entire floor of one of the old warehouses. They have a lot of room to themselves. Vladimir likes it that way, he says he is a modern man and modern men need to stretch out and be expansive.

The flat, however, is the only thing about Vladimir that is expansive. He lives a closely guarded and careful life. He has to stay out of sunshine and prefers to function at night. During the London summer this limits his lifestyle because in June the sun does not go down much before half past ten and then comes back up again very early. In the summer Vladimir and Mina go on holiday to the dark places of the southern hemisphere.

In the winter London is a night city and Vladimir is content and busy, rising in the afternoon as soon as the sun goes down. In December he is up as early as half past three. In the City he defines his own working hours.

Mina works with physically disabled children in an impoverished area of the East End of London. She has always considered herself left–wing and feminist and before she met Vladimir was involved in many different political struggles. She has spent years campaigning for the rights of the handicapped as well as the rights of the poor, the homeless, the powerless, and what she sees as the various victims of British Imperialism. Mina's grandmother was a Victorian lady who devoted her life to charity. Mina is proud of her heritage.

Vladimir claims that his ancestors were British aristocrats with Russian connections, hence his name and his impeccable accent. The night they met he told Mina he was the only child of parents long dead who left him a vast fortune which he had since made vaster. The fact that Vladimir was an orphan drew Mina towards him; it made him seem vulnerable. Never one to ignore an opportunity to comfort the bereaved, Mina insisted that Vladimir tell her his lonely life story. The tale was a bit thin on details but, despite that, Mina was charmed.

'This is the only photograph I have of her,' Vladimir said, producing from his breast pocket a sepia–tinted picture of a tall, slim and high–cheekboned woman dressed in a beaded shift, her hair in a marcel wave. 'She was young in this photo. It was taken years before she had me, her only child.' Mina could have kissed the picture and wept but instead she kissed Vladimir. His lips were very cool as was his skin but Mina assumed that was because of his class.

The next day Mina spoke to Eileen, one of her co-workers. 'You know my friend who works in the City?'

'You mean the one with the incredible car and the enormous salary?'

Mina nodded. 'I went to a party at her house last night

and I met the most extraordinary man. I spent the whole evening talking to him. He drove me home. Or rather, his chauffeur did. He didn't make a pass at me though, he showed me a photograph of his mother.'

'Sounds weird to me. Never trust a man who shows you a photo of his mum the first time you meet, that's what I always say.' Eileen tutted.

'He has black hair and long fingers and a very seductive smile. He is incredibly posh. I've never met anyone so posh.'

'Oh yeah, what's his name?'

'Vladimir.'

'Vladimir? That sounds foreign. Where does he come from?'

'Well, he is English . . .' Mina explained. The other woman said she didn't know what to think; the whole episode was very unlike Mina who was usually prone to having affairs with homeless immigrants and refugees who offered themselves to her like political sacrifices, sent from heaven to gratify Mina's curiosity about the barbaric world outside the East End of London.

That night when Mina finished work she stepped out the door of the building. Just as she was turning her collar against the wind she noticed the long black car. The passenger door opened and Vladimir stepped out. He waved at Mina and, after letting a car pass, walked across the street.

'Would you have dinner with me this evening?' he asked, his face pale under the streetlamp. Mina was flattered. She was unaccustomed to such flamboyant elegance and the interest of a rich man. She followed Vladimir back to his car, immediately worried about what she was wearing.

'I'm not dressed for anywhere smart,' she said covering her embarrassment with a laugh.

'You look wonderful,' he replied. 'I love a woman who has just been working.' Mina felt even more embarrassed. The car glided off through the night to a small Italian trattoria somewhere. They sat at a table in a dark corner and drank large glasses of full-bodied red wine. When the food arrived Mina noticed that Vladimir did not eat but she was so enthralled with the telling of her own life history that she did not think it worth interrupting. Usually men wanted to talk about themselves.

After the meal was finished, Vladimir smiled his handsome smile and said, in a low voice, 'Would you like to come and have coffee at my hotel?'

'Your hotel?' asked Mina, flustered. 'I thought you said you lived in London.'

'I'm looking for somewhere to buy.'

Mina smiled. By now she felt quite drunk. Vladimir's careful questions had made her feel clever and active, as if all the things she did were fascinating. Earlier she had tried to discover exactly what his business was. All he would say was that he took good care of his money.

They left the restaurant and got back into the car which had waited outside while they ate. On the wide black leather seat Vladimir pulled Mina's body close to his. She felt warm and excited and her mouth was dry with nervousness and anticipation. Vladimir kissed her on the neck. His cool lips felt unbearably soft and Mina let herself relax.

In his fifth-floor suite overlooking Hyde Park, Vladimir poured Mina another glass of wine and, as she raised it to her lips, unbuttoned her shirt. She put the glass back on the drinks table and let herself be undressed. He led her into the bedroom and laid her down on the bed. After taking off his own clothes he stretched out beside her, kissing her hair and her face. His lips travelled down her body and when he reached Mina's abdomen she tensed and said, 'I am bleeding.'

'I know,' he replied. Mina sank back into the pillows.

Not long after that Vladimir bought the flat in the docklands and Mina moved in with him. At night while Vladimir is away working Mina sits up and looks out their windows at the Thames which quietly slaps the concrete embankment below. The old refurbished ware-houses seem empty and lonely even though Mina knows all the flats have been bought by people like herself and Vladimir. Sometimes when the wind blows it is almost as if the area is derelict again, lifeless and without industry, the canals and wharves corrupt, decaying.

Vladimir's money buys Mina all sorts of things that she never knew she needed. It brings her warmth, freedom from bother, security and lots of space to be liberal in. Vladimir treats Mina well. He is faithful and amorous, especially when she menstruates. Things have always come easily to Vladimir. Mina thinks she might love him. He is tortured and sad and, beside him, all else pales away.

THE DINOSAURS
OF LOVE

In late October the sleet drives cold and hard in Toronto and at night the dark streets are slick and shiny with black ice. Magda found her feet would suddenly slide out from beneath her, as if about to take flight, as though each foot had voted for independence. The rest of her body would crumple and fall, thud, onto the hard sidewalk. Scraped, bruised, damp and cold, Magda thought a moment spent lying on the icy Toronto pavement was an eternity. In her heavy winter coat she felt like a woolly mammoth, entombed.

At night Magda dreamed she was lying on the icy ground when in fact she was lying in the arms of the Saint, her current boyfriend. Saint was long and bony and reptilian hard, his skin cool and a bit bumpy; Magda woke up on top of him, chilled. She rolled over and retrieved their cast-off duvet, rubbing her arms to get warm. She felt like a dinosaur, slow-witted and unwieldy. Saint slept on, unaware, and Magda dozed off again.

When she woke up next it was morning and Saint was already in the kitchen making coffee. He carried two mugs into the bedroom and got back into bed. Magda watched him lazily, eyeing his body which, although cold, she found exciting. 'I think,' murmured Saint, 'we should dress in matching clothing and wear our hearts on our sleeves. We'll start a new fashion.'

'In Toronto,' answered Magda, 'if you wore your heart on your sleeve it would freeze. Even a heart the size of a man would begin to beat sluggishly, the blood becoming ice-slushy, the tempo out of time. And matching clothes – we'd look like American tourists.'

'You are an American,' said Saint in his self-righteous Canadian way, as if simply being an American automatically conferred upon Magda some kind of moral depravity. Magda sipped her coffee and let his barb slide by, it found nothing to snag on her smooth skin. Saint ran his hand over her breast. His fingers felt freeze-dried; she shuddered.

After Magda lost in the quarter-finals at Wimbledon she gave up tennis, California, her cosmetic-surgery-addict of a mother, her Porsche, her tennis coach husband, five million dollars' worth of product endorsement contracts, her pasta machine, and her monthly peroxide treatments. Early one morning, before even the army of Los Angeles cleaning ladies were awake, she took a cab to the empty airport and, rubbing sleep from her eyes, bought a ticket to somewhere she had never been. Canada meant very little to her then, somewhere north, big, and far away. It was not that she had felt humiliated at Wimbledon or that she had in any way been disgraced; it was more that she had suddenly felt totally and obnoxiously bored. Perhaps it had been something that Veronica, her dancer friend in London, had said that triggered her decision. That story about the ballerina who had faked a brain tumour for sympathy and then died anyway had seemed so inexplicable; it made Magda feel tired and drained. In the face of such gargantuan self-deception, everything else looked silly and futile. And Veronica herself was so cynical and worn out; she and Magda had gone to the cinema and argued about the facts of life. After that the thought of hitting yet another tennis ball back and forth over a net made her own brain ache. Magda had never really liked professional tennis; that, along with the blonde hair, had been her mother's idea. 'That's it,' she said to herself on the plane. 'I'm gone.'

In Toronto she told no one about her previous career and, dressed in black with her dark roots growing in, no one recognized her. After daily workouts at the YMCA she applied her careful, thick make-up (she continued to feel a need for disguise) and went out on the cold, windy streets. Toronto was not like California. Even the city's plans to cover over one of the small islands in Lake Ontario and create a mini-Florida did not make it more like California. The stock exchange that mimicked Wall Street and the fact that everyone knew Mickey Mouse did not make Canada American either and Magda felt pleased by this. The bizarre Canadianness of Saint made her happy as well. Once they moved in together she felt she almost belonged; at least, she belonged to him.

In Eastern Canada the autumn is marked by the fall of leaves from the trees. Green becomes red, yellow and orange, gold stands out starkly against the black and bark of the beeches. Magda had not expected this marvel at the grey end of summer and felt overwhelmed. She looked at Saint with new respect. You live through this agony of death and regeneration every year, she thought, as she lay next to his cold, hard body. While the cups of coffee iced over she and Saint made love and, afterward, he fell asleep again. Every year the leaves fall orange and red, splattered with blood and Hallowe'en, and your life as Saint continues without pausing, and the lives of other Saints like you do as well.

As the trees changed, Magda was changing too. She moved through the streets of the frozen, uptight city less aggressively than at first, more willing to fall behind. She often walked along Bloor Street and, crossing the Humber river, would stare from the high bridge down at the water as it snaked its way through the colours. She rode the subway with reluctance preferring the more stately and scenic progression of the streetcars. The air was laden with autumnal longing; the whole city seemed to be waiting. Magda wondered if people were simply cooling down after the hot summer, stalling and lingering until the first snowfall came and laid its winter weight on their shoulders.

Still able to afford not to work – if nothing else, her tennis career had been lucrative – Magda spent hours sitting in Polish cafés reading novels. On the days Saint had off from the restaurant – he was a chef – they visited art galleries, exhibitions and bookshops. They went to the Royal Ontario Museum and spent a long time lingering over the dinosaurs. Saint became expansive. He kept swearing softly and exclaiming, 'I wonder how they had sex?' over the bones. With her woollen hat, gloves and scarf temporarily stored in the cloakroom, Magda, however, could think only of the approaching ice-age; she thought it must have felt as baffling and inexplicable then as it did now.

At night Magda and Saint slept with the bedroom window open. Saint claimed the room was too hot and he needed the fresh air in order to maintain his low body temperature. Magda curled up and willed her pulse to slow. Outside the wind blew and sometimes leaves were swept in through the billowing curtains. Purple, gold, and brown, they stuck to the wall opposite like prints made by schoolchildren. Seeing this, Magda felt like a little girl, thrilled by discovery. In the blue morning light she nudged Saint and said, 'Wake up.'

Saint moaned. He was dreaming. Magda kissed him and held his head in her hands. He opened his eyes.

'Let's get married,' Magda said plainly.

'Married?' said Saint. 'That's for dinosaurs. It's an out-moded institution.'

'Let's do it anyway. Let's do it for T–Rex.'

Saint gathered Magda into his spiny arms. 'You're always so hot,' he said. Then he looked into her eyes and she felt him thaw a little. 'Okay,' he said, 'let's get married.'

'Till death do us part,' said Magda.

'We'll face extinction together,' he added, 'you and me.'

IRISES

I

VIOLET

I can't stop thinking about her.

We met in a pub, not a student place, but somewhere a bit different, where real people go after they finish real jobs. My friends and I wanted an evening away from college, from libraries, from books. Not that we didn't have evenings off, we had lots of evenings off. In fact, evenings off were a way of life for us. We trooped down to the pub, our wallets slim, because students are poor; even students who, unlike me, are from wealthy families, get very poor when it comes to a night out at the pub.

She was there, and I watched her for a bit, then Geoff, my friend from Birmingham – the longer he stayed in Cambridge, the thicker his Brummy accent became – Geoff went up to her and started talking. Turned out he knew her, he'd met her at some bar or another, student party, or something. She was a little undergraduate, I should have known by looking at her, she had that thin, under-twenty look, but I was too taken in by it all, by her, by her glossy long hair, and her pale blue-veined skin. I went over and joined them, and Geoff took his time about introducing us, but he did eventually. Her name was Iris. I couldn't believe it. Iris. Like the flower. Like the dark purple colour of her eyes, of her . . . irises. It makes me hold my breath to think of her eyes. Iris.

And these were her first words to me: 'Bill,' she said, 'do you understand this place?'

I looked around. Did she mean the pub?

'Well . . .' I said, hesitating, not wanting to get this, our first exchange, wrong.

'I mean, they told me Cambridge was a famous university, but they didn't tell me Cambridge was famous for being weird.'

Weird. Of course, she was right, it was weird, deeply weird. I knew that, but I had got used to it somehow, used to the colleges and the formal dinners and the academic gowns and the supervisions with the dons who fell asleep while you talked to them. That actually happened to me when I was an undergraduate. Dr Simms, the man who was meant to be imparting great knowledge unto me, Dr Simms, my supervisor, fellow of St Paul's College, recipient of two honorary doctorates, expert in his field, Dr Simms fell asleep while I read my paper. I could have killed him. Perhaps I should have killed him and done countless other hopeful and anxious students a service.

But, instead, I stayed on, intent on getting my doctorate and maybe one day falling asleep in supervisions of my own.

The other thing about her was, of course, that she was foreign, she was American, so she might have meant the pub, that wouldn't have been far-fetched, it is weird to have to get your own drinks from the bar and to stand, to stand all evening, in the midst of the fake sawdust and the cigarette smoke. She was here on a scholarship, a big fucking scholarship, can you believe it? And she was standing next to me. Geoff had disappeared. I will always love him for that.

'Iris,' I said, 'you're absolutely right. It is weird. It is entirely weird.' And I laughed and she laughed with me.

And then three months later I killed her. And a week after that, I chopped her up. I had to get rid of her body somehow. And by then it was no longer her, no longer Iris in any sense that I could recognize.

Things went well in the pub that night. We liked each other. She had been in Cambridge, in England, for only one month, and I suspect that back in the US she'd seen too many Merchant Ivory films, read too much Evelyn Waugh and Graham Greene, paid too much attention to Hugh Grant and Daniel Day-Lewis for her own good. She thought English men were sexy. I was lucky, she'd been here too little time to be disabused of that. And, I admit, I was on good form that night, I had just that day had my hair cut so unfashionably short that I looked like I was on the edge of some new trend, I'd remembered to shave before coming out, I looked clean-cut, trustworthy, honourable, maybe even a bit American. At the time, I would have liked to have been an American. I told jokes, she laughed at them. She confided in me, after another couple of pints. She told me she wasn't overly impressed with the quality of teaching at the university, in fact, she was shocked by the way they did things here. She'd heard one too many academics say that their real work, the important stuff, was their own research, not teaching. I told her my story about Dr Simms.

I didn't make any mistakes, didn't make a fool of myself. We parted ways at half past eleven, she off to her college, me off to the flat I shared with Geoff and Raj and

Tim. I slept like a log that night, I always slept well after evenings out, my head full of Iris and beer instead of books, papers, and all the work I should be doing and was not.

In the morning I opened my eyes and realized I had forgotten to ask what college she was at. I got out of bed and caught Geoff before he headed off to the library. Then I spent the morning writing a note, composing a note, writing her a brief letter asking if she would consider going out with me on Thursday. We had met on Monday – Thursday seemed soon, but not too soon, and Friday, well, it was a risk asking a woman out on the weekend. I don't know why I thought that, I can't remember the reasoning behind that particular theory, it was probably something Geoff had told me and I had taken as gospel since Geoff was one year older than me and always had a string of new and glorious girlfriends. The trick seemed to be to restrict first dates to week nights. And I am never one to question received wisdom.

So I asked Iris if she would like to meet me at the pub, the same pub, the same auspicious pub, on Thursday night at nine p.m. Late enough to get some work done beforehand, late enough so that if we hate each other we can say we need to get home and do some more work. Early enough that we'll have time to drink too much so that we can carry on carrying on elsewhere. Sometimes I sound just like my dad.

Disposing of her body was incredibly difficult. It made sense to do it, I'd killed her and logic dictated that in order to prevent myself from getting caught I had to get rid of the body. At first I thought I could just keep her with me. That way, she would never be found, and without a body, there could be no evidence. When the bedder came round to clean my room, I pretended we were asleep. I told Geoff and Raj and Tim she had a cold and that I was taking care of her. But, of course, I wasn't thinking straight, and after a week, even in Cambridge where my room was so cold that some mornings I'd wake up and find frost on the inside of the windows, she began to smell. We began to smell. So I waited until the weekend, when everyone was going away.

Iris was at the pub already when I got there on Thursday night, even though I was a good fifteen minutes early. She was alone, she hadn't brought anyone with her, no friends to make things easier. She wasn't a timid girl and I liked that. She bought the first round. We found seats, it seemed like a miracle at the time. One seat, a wooden bench that required us to sit right next to each other, our thighs pushed together like sausages in plastic wrapping. Nobody that we knew came into the pub, another miracle. We were left on our own, with each other.

We talked about America, she told me about the small town where she grew up. New Hampshire, big wooden houses with verandas and lawns that lead to sidewalks that lead to schools and fire stations and the local library. I tried to picture it, she said it was like *Our Town*, which I hadn't read. 'Think of a movie,' I said, 'think of a movie with a town like your town.'

She laughed. '*Blue Velvet*,' she said, 'only safe and nice and calm.'

We drank quite a lot, quickly. 'I never really drink at home,' she said. 'But here everything seems to revolve around alcohol.'

'We don't have to drink,' I said, and then I wondered

what I meant. I had been looking forward to getting drunk with her. 'I mean, next time, next time we meet, we won't drink, we'll do something wholesome and fun. What do healthy Americans do for fun?'

'Have sex,' she said, smiling, and I wasn't shocked. But the plastic around our sausages suddenly felt a little tighter.

I don't know, I think she must have been very lonely. I got lonely, and I'm English, I'd lived in Cambridge for five years, I knew loads of people, someone was always coming around, dropping by, arranging parties and outings and weekends away. She was only eighteen, she'd never been away from home before, and she was very clever, very intelligent, 'smart', as she'd say, smart and sharp. It couldn't have been easy, being new to university and new to the country all at the same time. And we hit if off. She didn't show me her loneliness, but I could see it. It shone around her like a halo.

I walked her back to her college. The wind was hoary and penetrating and we hurried along the pavement. After a while I realized she was mumbling, almost under her breath – 'St John's, Trinity, Gonville and Caius' – she pronounced Caius incorrectly, like 'cay-us' instead of 'keys' – 'Trinity Hall, Clare . . .' As we walked along past the big medieval walls she named the colleges, as if this would help us on our way. I was too drunk to think this odd, and it was too cold to talk. On Clare Bridge she took my hand. She took off her glove and drew my hand out of my pocket, my bare hand, I never wore gloves, I could never keep track of them for more than a day. Her fingers felt strong and long and her palm slid warmly against mine. Then she put our hands into my pocket, both of them, and they remained there, locked together, knocking against my hip as we strode along the dark street.

At her college, I walked her to the door. She looked wonderful as she turned to me.

'Good-night,' she said.

'Good-night,' I replied, and we kissed as though it was perfectly natural. And I wandered home, warm and excited and pleased.

On Sunday we had arranged to walk to Grantchester, but when she arrived at my place to pick me up, it was raining. We debated whether or not we were hardy enough to go anyway, and decided against it. We made mugs of tea and went up to my room. It wasn't too awful – when I saw the weather I had anticipated this and done some tidying – and we sat on the floor in front of the gas fire and talked. I had a fairly large room at the back of a house owned by the college. It was quiet, outside winter birds called, and in the distance, on the green, they were playing rugby and from time to time we could hear that as well. It got dark just after five, and I made more tea, and we ended the afternoon lying on my bed, side by side, our clothes on, touching.

You know, I wasn't a virgin. Of course not, I was twenty-four by then. I was fairly successful with girls, although not as popular as Geoff, but he was a Sex Addict, we used to tell him he needed counselling. I was a nice young man, I liked women, I liked the way they smelt, and talked, and worried, the way they could be just like blokes when they wanted, then like an alien species at other times. Some men at Cambridge, es-pecially the public-school boys who hadn't gone to school with girls, who'd lived away from their mothers and sisters from a tender age, couldn't seem to catch on to how to relate to the opposite sex, but I didn't have that problem. I had two sisters, you see, and they were older and brighter and braver than me, and when I was young I wanted to be more like them. Iris said she found me easy to talk to. She sat up on my bed, and said, 'Hey, you're easy to talk to, for an English guy, I feel relaxed for the first time in ages.' I took this as a great compliment. And I took it as an opportunity to grasp her arm, pull her down close to me, and kiss her on the lips once again.

Her body was very white, unlined, and lovely, even after she was dead. There was a mole on her left breast, it had become so familiar, like a signpost that told me I was in the right place. She was quite hairy, dark hair on her arms and her legs, but I liked that, I had luxuriated in her pubic hair and what was buried beneath it. I carried her into the bathroom a couple of hours after everyone left the house. I was well prepared, I'd bought a whole roll of black rubbish bags, and I'd stolen a saw from the garden store in the grounds of the college. I climbed over the fence the night before. I was frightened, but it proved easy to get one of the windows of the shed to open, it had been left slightly ajar. Inside there was an array of saws, as well as axes and hammers, and I took a smaller, sharp-toothed one that I thought would do the job. I wasn't expert at this, no way. I didn't even eat meat.

Iris was a vegetarian too, we had that in common. I knew a bit about the US, the guns, the celebrities, a little history. And she knew nothing about England, absolutely nothing. Sometimes it was as if we weren't even speaking the same language. Being with her made Britain seem so insignificant, in a way I hadn't quite fathomed before. And it is insignificant, it's a pissant little country swilling about in its own shit, dreaming of better days. Sometimes I think it's an indication of where we are at that we still think Cambridge is one of our best universities. Half the decent people who were here when I arrived have left for posts in the US. The entire History faculty seems desperate to leave. Except the old guys, of course, except for the old men like Dr Simms. And there are plenty of them, old at heart, if not in years.

When we made love it was a complete revelation. I don't know, I guess I'd never done it and fallen in love at the same time before. With other girls I had always struggled to get it right the first time, and with her, it simply was right. It couldn't have been more right. And at the end there was a fabulous reward in it for me: the way she came. She kept her eyes open the whole time, her purple eyes looked right into me without glazing over, without losing focus in her reverie. And when she came she grabbed hold of me as though it was me who she wanted, only me, and she would want only me forever. She said my name and gasped, her breath deep and harsh. And my own orgasm was like a swoon. I sank into her and never wanted to resurface.

From then on we were an item, we were a romance, and we fell into habits and ways that were familiar to us from all the other student loves by which we were surrounded. Except with Iris I felt completely different from all the rest, with Iris I felt as though I had been blessed. I am not a religious person, but I felt beatified, deified, sainted. She was the best of me. We spent a lot of time together, although Iris had her friends, and she kept up with them, she was a good friend, a good person. I kept up with Geoff and Raj and Tim, I lived with them, we had no choice. We all had girlfriends at that point, which was highly unusual, and the house had an enticing sex-fug that permeated the very walls between our bedrooms. We were trememdously relaxed and pleased with ourselves. On the nights the girls were out and we were in, we cooked for each other, ribbed each other, drank cans of lager, and went to bed early.

In the bathtub, Iris's body looked small, deflated and rigid at the same time. I didn't know where to start. I picked up her left foot, the heel cupped in my hand, and her whole body lifted stiffly, like a Barbie Doll. She had clean little feet, and her toenails were evenly clipped, unpainted. I placed the saw just above her ankle, pushed it back and forth once or twice. There was a trickle of blood, not much. Her heart was no longer pumping.

I'd seen Iris's blood before. About two weeks after we'd started sleeping together, she got her period. Some girls are very squeamish about menstruating, it's as if they think men don't know that this is what happens to women. They behave as though we might suddenly go off them when we find out they bleed. But Iris wasn't like that. She was totally matter of fact, complaining. It came in the middle of the night, and in those first few hours it was evident that she was in a fair amount of pain. She said the best cure for it was sex. She got on top of me and moved back and forth very slowly. We weren't using a condom and we got very messy, blood all over the sheets. But I felt that blood was our ritual bonding, as though we were two kids who had sliced our thumbs and pressed them together. It felt like an enormous, mutual exchange.

We had an amazing month together. We both worked really hard. Iris was academically ambitious, and I got more done than I had during the entire previous year. She was reading English Literature and at night sometimes she would read to me, bits of Chaucer, passages from Milton, Shakespeare. It was funny hearing this stuff in her New England accent, and she would ham it up, to make me laugh. On days when the sun shone we'd go out on the river; she'd lie elegantly back in the punt and I'd stand at the rear with the pole, singing operatic arias that I made up on the spot. Sometimes in the middle of the night, we'd sneak into my college's brand-new library. We'd have sex on a chair, fully dressed, surrounded by books, the blue light from the computer terminals on our backs and faces.

And then term ended and Iris went home for Christmas. At Cambridge terms are very short, eight weeks, and the break stretches for more than six. I went with her to Heathrow, I had to work very hard not to get upset, and she was so light-hearted, looking forward to seeing her family, her dog, her friends. Her life in America was suddenly real to me, and I found it unbearable that she should have something so far beyond my reach. When she went through passport control and passed out of my sight, I sat down on the steps, right there, in front of the tie shop and the book shop and the place for coffee. People moved around me as though I was a turnstile, an empty baggage trolley.

Getting through the bones was difficult, but I had anticipated that. I had taken off my clothes and covered every surface with plastic carrier bags. We always had so many carrier bags in the kitchen, as though we collected them specially. Very quickly I was coated in blood. Slippery. There was nothing sexual in it, how could there be? Yet I found what I was doing possessed great intimacy. She was small, but she had been strong, and there was the rigor mortis. I had known her body well, and now I knew it better.

Christmas passed without drama. I stayed in Cambridge until Christmas Eve, and then went home to Leicester on the train. On Boxing Day my family and I went to Bobby's for a curry. We sat upstairs and the metal tumblers made my teeth sting. They still had the Diwali lights up along the street. Afterwards, in the car on the way back to the house my sister Susan, the eldest, announced that she was getting married.

'Who to?' my mother cried, craning around in the front seat.

'Jeremy,' my sister replied calmly. She was sitting between me and Liz.

'That ponce,' Liz said under her breath. Susan rounded on her.

'What did you call him?' she asked, raising her fist.

Liz started to smile. 'A ponce,' she said, laughing. 'I'm sorry.' Susan punched her on her arm, hard. Liz screamed ouch, ow, ouch, laughing as Susan continued to hit her.

'Girls!' said my mother, and then she looked at my father, and they also began to laugh.

When we got home we had a party, we had been drunk for the better part of two days anyway. That night, when we went to bed, I sneaked into my sisters' room with my blankets and pillow and slept on the floor between them like I used to when I was a kid. In the middle of the night I woke to the sound of their even, measured breathing.

I went back to Cambridge before New Year and settled in to work, and to waiting for Iris's return from the US. It wasn't a bad time. Geoff and Raj and Tim were there, and their girlfriends, and they felt sorry for me and bought me drinks and made me offerings of cakes and biscuits. In the thin-walled house it was not uncommon to overhear these couples having sex, and sometimes at my desk I would look up, out the window at the dark afternoon, and try to figure out who it was I could hear. I didn't mind, it made me look forward to Iris.

During this time I received one letter from her, one only. It came in a scented envelope with matching lavender paper, which seemed childish, but also endearing. She did not say much, just that things were well, there was a lot of snow, she had been to Vermont to ski. She signed the note, 'with love', and I pondered over that for a long while. I think if she had signed it 'Love' I would have been happier. But these are the kinds of things people like me dwell on, people who are young, besotted, and sweaty.

I took the coach from Cambridge to Heathrow to meet her. Her plane was late, but I continued to wait with the crowd by the doors of the arrival lounge, I didn't want to miss her. It was strange watching reunion after reunion take place – families, young couples, elderly men returning home from visiting their children who had emigrated, gone away. It must have been hard to come back to Britain when your kids lived in Florida. Maybe I would emigrate, maybe I would marry Iris and we would go live in Texas, or New York, or LA. Or perhaps we'd stay in Cambridge, I would give supervisions, and my lover would continue to be very brilliant for all her days.

Finally, it was Iris who emerged from behind the glass partition. She had a lot of baggage, big American suitcases and travel bags. She was wearing a woolly hat, and a backpack, and her face was burnt and tanned from skiing. She looked young, and somehow incomplete, like she had got out of the baking tray before she was finished. I felt hesitant then, after my onanistic excesses of the past six weeks – was it this girl, this Iris, that I loved, or some kind of phantom girl I had conjured up, based on Iris, but not Iris in any substantial way?

She saw me and came forward, put her hand on my cheek, drew my face down to hers, and kissed me. My doubts fled. On the coach we sat at the back and I tried to get Iris to have sex with me, right there and then, but she didn't want it. I was desperate to see that look on her face once again, to show myself I had not imagined it. She wanted to talk, so we talked; she told me about her friends, about what they had done together. She was full of America, full of the way she lived there, as though she wasn't sure what she was doing here, back in England, as though she was suddenly going to be very homesick indeed. Iris didn't come from money, her family was solidly middle class, but her life in the US sounded materially much richer than mine in the UK, outdoor sports, horses, lots of TVs. 'I was sad to leave my car behind,' she said, and I thought I could understand what she meant, if I had a car I'd be sad to leave it too.

When it came down to it, I couldn't carry out what I had planned. It went all right, the saw, the cutting, when I was dealing with arms and legs. They were portable somehow, the shin-bone disconnected from the ankle-bone, etc., like a new kind of Lego. Soon I had a pile of black sacks near the door and, in the bathtub, less and less of Iris. Not that I thought of the body as Iris. As I mentioned before, there were the familiar markings, but by now there was so much blood and gore that she was mostly unrecognizable. Of course, I was left with her torso and her head. I didn't know what to do. I couldn't face sawing it up, her breasts, her ribs, her navel. And I was not able to decapitate her. I know I should have, it was logical, the smaller the pieces, the better. But I couldn't do it. I didn't have it in me. So I put what was left of her, my Iris, in yet another black rubbish bag, and set about cleaning the bathroom.

The first week that she was back was great. The moment we got off the coach it was as though she came back to life, as though she realized she was in Cambridge, not still in the US or some halfway place in the air between. She rushed around her college, knocking on doors, leaving notes, embracing her friends who had themselves just returned from the holidays. I waited for her in her room, lying on her bed, content to breathe in the smell of her things. I hadn't spent much time in her room before, her college kept an unofficial but watchful eye over its members' nocturnal activities. But this was the afternoon, and no one was going to ask me why I was there.

When Iris came back into the room, her cheeks were flushed, and she was smiling and happy. She closed the door, locked it, and leapt on top of me. Getting back inside her could not have made me happier. Nothing else could make me feel as complete. And she kept her eyes on me, just like in my dreams, her purple eyes, her Iris eyes, looking right at me.

We had a good time. Lots of socializing, lots of sex, a lot of work. We spent most of our day together, and every night. Iris did seem a little different, but I put that down to the weeks we had spent apart, which, I realized, was more time than we had actually spent together. I figured I had mythologized her a little, and I needed to adjust to the real thing.

The second week of term wasn't so good. Iris had an argument with Geoff. We were sitting around in the kitchen, drinking lager. He'd been slagging off the US, slagging off Americans in general, going on about their foreign policy, what they had done and were doing in Cuba and Central America. Iris clearly didn't know anything about Central America, neither did I, but she was angry. I could see he was goading her, that he wanted to show that she was fundamentally ignorant about her own country, implying that the situation down there was somehow her fault, the fault of all Americans like her. I tried to intervene, but that infuriated her even more. Iris stood up, and announced that she was leaving. I couldn't believe it, I wanted to hit Geoff, I wanted Iris to sit down and stay. But instead of doing something manly and convincing, I burst into tears. Everyone turned and looked, shock on their faces. And then they all laughed at me, and the tension dissipated.

Later, Iris and I got into bed. I guess I was fairly demanding as a boyfriend, but I couldn't help myself, being near her made me incredibly horny. Iris pushed me away. She sat up in the darkness and pulled her jumper down over her breasts. 'Look,' she said, I remember her words so clearly, 'while I was home I met someone else.'

I couldn't speak. My eyes still ached a little from earlier, and I felt fresh tears spring to the surface, like blood to an old wound.

'I knew him in high school, but he's been away like me, and he's really different.' She turned to me as though she expected me to be interested.

'He's my age,' she added.

Which made me feel old, and somehow dirty. I managed to speak. 'Yes?' I said. 'That doesn't mean we have to change, does it?'

She was silent, as though she was turning the thought over in her head. 'I guess not,' she said. 'I'm here, after all, and he isn't.' She lay back down. 'And you are here,' she said, 'aren't you?' Iris made love to me then, very carefully.

I had done a good job with the carrier bags in the bathroom and I found cleaning up relatively easy. I washed down the walls, every crevice and crack, I'd read too many crime novels to be careless. I gave myself a good bath as well, and emerged feeling cleaner than I had in ages. I put all the black rubbish sacks, including the big one, into my carry-all. I carried the bag to my room, got dressed, went out into the street. By then it was very late. I thought about riding my bicycle, but decided the carry-all would be too unwieldly. I walked across the green to the Cam. The load was very heavy. One by one I dropped the bags into the river. It was like delivering newspapers, a few hundred feet, drop another, the burden lessening. I walked away from the colleges, along the river. Cambridge is incredibly dark, women students are always complaining, and I'd had some pretty scary trips across town at night myself, but tonight I was glad of it. I figured nothing could happen to me that was worse than what I'd done. When I was finished I dumped the carry-all and took the saw back to the college.

So term went on, Iris and I kept going, kept seeing each other, as though nothing had changed. I made her tell me the gory details, perhaps that was my mistake. She had slept with this guy, whose name was Joe, and I found that knowledge made me perform with her, sexually, all the better, all the more desperately, dramatically. It was as though by penetrating her more deeply, by making her come more frequently, loudly, I would somehow strengthen my claim on her. We drove my housemates crazy, we were always banging away, quite literally, my head, or Iris's foot, drumming against the wall. That's all we did those weeks, studied and fucked, fucked and studied, there wasn't time for much else.

But then Iris's eyes began to glaze over. I was going down on her one afternoon and I looked up, looked at her sweet face, and saw her eyes had gone out of focus. She was gazing at the ceiling, not seeing anything, not seeing me. I knew she was thinking about her other man. But I carried on as though I had noticed nothing.

I didn't sleep very well the night after I dropped Iris in the Cam. The next morning I got on my bike and went down to the river. All the sacks had disappeared, except one, the big one. It was bobbing up and down right in front of a college boathouse. I cycled back into the centre of town, and hired a punt. I poled down the river. Some friends of mine were walking along the bank and they called out to me and stood on their tiptoes as though expecting to see Iris lying in the boat. I waved and thought it best not to offer any explanation. I reached the rubbish bag and steered the boat right towards it. There was a horrible smack when it hit the prow. I manoeuvred the boat around the sack, and punctured the plastic with the pole. As the bag filled with water, it sank. I was so relieved I nearly passed out.

Iris kept on mispronouncing the names of the colleges and streets in Cambridge, names like Caius, Magdalene. First it was a kind of joke, and then we all started doing it, Geoff and Raj and Tim and their girlfriends, and soon it became part of the way we spoke. It was fun, it felt like we'd created our own language. And as the days passed our relationship grew more and more frenetic.

Until suddenly it stopped. It just stopped. Iris looked at me, and I could see she didn't want me. After Christmas she had loved me less, but she had still loved me. But now even that was gone. I couldn't believe it. How could she stop loving me? How could she simply turn around and stop?

I should have retreated immediately. I should have been dignified and restrained and become distant and aloof – stolen the fire from her. But I didn't. I began to follow her, not like a stalker, but like a puppy dog. Every time she moved, I was there, wagging my tail, tongue hanging out. She'd give me a nice smile and walk away.

It was like being a junkie and losing my dealer. It was like being an alcoholic deprived of drink. I knew it was bad for me.

And, can you believe it, the worst thing, the worst thing of all, was doing without sex. Was living without fucking Iris. Surviving without that grace and faith, that generosity and beauty.

★

Of course I knew they would catch me. I reported her missing, and I cried a lot in the police station, but they knew it was me, and I knew they knew. To my horror – and everyone else's – they dredged the river. They found her hands – that was all, her hands, everything else had disappeared. A supermarket clerk made a statement saying I had bought the black rubbish sacks. Geoff told the police about the missing carrier bags.

The trial will soon be over.

She fought hard. I knew she would. She was small, yet she was strong, but we were not evenly matched. I found it easy to do. It occurred to me one moment, and the next, it was done. People are quite fragile really, when you think about it. They die very quickly, one minute full of struggle, the next absolutely still.

The thing they are saying about me in the papers is how normal I appear. How perfectly ordinary – rather handsome, in fact, intelligent, from a nice family. Everyone is saying how they would never have thought me capable of such a thing – such an overpowering love, and such violence. But I am capable of it, and not simply because Iris made me so. I am capable of it. We all are.

We just have to find the right person.

2

WHAT WAS IT LIKE?

I read somewhere that the long-term girlfriend of the handsome American serial killer, Ted Bundy, once woke up in the middle of the night to find Ted huddled under the sheets with a flashlight, examining her body. She didn't dump him. A little while later she went to the police and told them she thought her boyfriend was the same 'Ted' as the one reputed to have killed thirty-six women, all of whom had hair just like hers, long, brown, and parted in the middle. Even then she couldn't bring herself to show him the door.

I'm not like that. I would have given him the boot. I am not the kind of woman who hangs on just for the sake of hanging on. For instance, I would not tolerate abuse. Whatever its nature – physical, mental – whatever. If any bloke even threatened to hit me, I'd be gone. I would know if my boyfriend was a murderer.

In fact, my boyfriend is a murderer. This is proven. He admitted his guilt from the start. As soon as they took him into custody, as soon as he could see that they knew, he told the truth. He admitted his guilt and they put him in prison, they gave him a life sentence, because that is what you get for murder in this country, regardless of whom you kill, your girlfriend, your wife, or a complete stranger. And he served his whole sentence – of course, life doesn't mean life, and nor should it. He served thirteen and a half years and in that time he was an ideal prisoner. He finished his doctorate. He wrote his thesis in his cell. It took them a while to get around to it, but eventually he was awarded his degree. It proved too difficult to continue with his research after that – history – so he did another BA, an English Literature degree through the Open University. Things are slow in prison, time moves lethargically. He went to the gym regularly, he kept to himself, and got on well enough with both screws and fellow prisoners. He didn't need to be reformed, he already was reformed, he killed a young American woman named Iris and went to prison, he wasn't about to repeat the performance. And he was more intelligent than most people who work in the prison service. Despite successive government crackdowns on prisons, the average length of a life sentence is still thirteen, going on fourteen, years. And that's what Bill served.

We met because I was looking for something worthwhile to do, so I became a volunteer prison visitor. It's a scheme for prisoners who need befriending; a lot of men lose everything when they get banged up. They've killed their women, and their children are taken away, and their families are too ashamed to visit. Bill wasn't like that, he didn't have children and his family kept in contact, but still, he was lonely. We began to correspond and I started visiting.

I am not like one of those American women. Before the lights dimmed in Tallahassee when they electrocuted Ted Bundy, he had amassed a large and devoted female following. Women were always writing to him, saying they loved him, sending him things – their knickers, for God's sake. He killed more than thirty-six women, and they loved him! Ted got married during his trial, although not to his long-term girlfriend, by that time she had left him. He and his wife conceived a child in prison – not during a conjugal visit, they didn't have such things, but in the toilet after Ted Bundy had bribed the guards to leave them alone for five minutes. What was that woman thinking – did she get off on the fact that her husband was on Death Row? I am not like that – that's ghoulish. There is nothing like that about me.

The first time I went to the prison to meet Bill was fine. I had been in a couple of times before, to see another man I'd befriended, who had since been released. I looked normal, I didn't get dressed up, I didn't want to look like I needed to impress, I wanted to look ordinary. The way some of the women dress, they should put up a sign at the entrance – Don't Tease The Prisoners. I am a schoolteacher, I teach teenage boys, so I know what they are like, and a lot of men in prison are very young. But Bill is not a teenager, and neither am I. When he came into the visits room, I felt a little bad about the fact that I hadn't dressed up. His prison clothes were so carefully pressed. We shook hands, and thanked each other for the letters we'd been writing. I went to the canteen and bought tea and KitKats, and we sat down and started to try to be friends. It is a very artificial situation, prison visiting. It is difficult to behave anything like you would do normally. Bill was nervous, and so was I.

In my social circle it is not unusual that I am thirty-three and not married. I've had long-term boyfriends, but I used to think I wouldn't get married, that marriage as an institution was bad for women. I don't go to church, so I wouldn't get married for religious reasons. My parents have never got on all that well, so they are not a great advertisement for it either. Cambridge is not a big town, and among the parents and school governors attitudes differ, but generally, people do live in the modern world. Yet I've met plenty of men who think it's strange that I'm not married, that I've never been married, that somehow my great age endows me with a kind of dried-toast spinsterhood. I was glad to see Bill wasn't like that.

And really, he was just like anyone else, except perhaps someone who'd been away for a while. He was up on everything, all the latest TV, books, music, films, even though he hadn't watched, read, heard, or been to anything – he consumed the available newspapers very diligently. That was one thing I began to do right away, give him my old newspapers instead of recycling them. He knew a lot about politics, about current affairs, and that's always been one of my interests too. We were both avid consumers of Radio 4. And yet, like I said, he had this strange distance from the world, as though he spent his days looking at it through binoculars, studying a little bit at a time. I guess that's only natural after a decade inside.

When we met, Bill was coming up to the stage when they begin to let prisoners back into the world. He was going to be eligible for home leave, for the odd day-trip. Every prisoner is different and he wasn't going to be sent to an open prison. For some reason he was still consid-ered Category B, a little dangerous, but not an A-man. He might be allowed breaths of fresh air, maybe once or twice a year. I think getting to know me was a conscious decision he made, a way of easing himself back into the outside. As we got to know and began to trust each other, he told me that one of the reasons he had replied to my letter was that he thought if he could form a friendship with a woman like me the parole board might look on him more favourably. I wasn't shocked by that, I understood that in prison you do what you must to survive. I understood that he wanted to get out.

At first we kept our lives quite separate. He told me a little about his family, I told him a little about mine. I tried to keep it normal, to treat him like I would anyone, not hiding anything, but not being too forward either. Mostly we wrote and talked about books and the radio – we began to co-ordinate our reading and our listening. And after corresponding weekly for more than a year, after we'd had several visits, I began to find Bill in my thoughts at odd moments, at school when I watched the boys running in the playing field, the way they'd shout and jump and stretch. Out in the evening with my friends, around a table in a restaurant, passing the bottle of wine, listening to Elise tell her wild stories about her misspent youth. At Christmas with my parents in Brighton. I found myself thinking how much Bill would enjoy these things. And knowing he couldn't began to spoil my pleasure. This realization came upon me slowly, and was sweet.

I started to visit more often. We confided in each other more deeply. His letters used to arrive in the morning post. I'd pick them up on my way out to work, and it got so that I didn't feel comfortable reading in the staffroom, I'd wait until I got back to the privacy of my flat in the evening. In the spring, eighteen months after we met – I remember the day clearly – I received the letter in which he told me what he had done. What crime he had committed, how he ended up in prison, instead of shored up in some Cambridge college like everyone had expected. The letter came out of the blue, I had never asked him to explain himself. It seemed too private a thing, the way there too dark, for me to ask about it.

The wording of the letter was very concise.

Dear Laura,
I killed my American girlfriend Iris because I was jealous of her, and she no longer loved me. I was angry, I was hurt, I

*was shaking her, then she was gone. I am guilty of murder. I
had a perfect life with my friends and my studies and the pubs
and the football, and I dumped Iris and all of that in the river.
I do not deserve to be forgiven, perhaps I don't deserve to live.
But I am alive, I am here on this planet, and I have to find a
way to be in this world. Your friendship is very important to
me.*

He went on, and I was glad that I was at home, because
I found myself shivering.

That night it took me a long time to fall asleep. Of
course I had known that Bill was a murderer, he was
serving a life sentence. It was in the back of my mind all
the time when we first met, but as we had grown closer,
that thought had slipped away. His letter made me ask
myself all kinds of questions – what is the difference
between Bill and me? Why is he a murderer, and I'm not?
Could I be? Could he do it again? What was it like? What
was Iris like? What would she be like now if she were still
alive? Those questions kept me awake for a long time,
but when I woke up in the dark I woke because I had
remembered something.

I remembered when they dredged the river. I remembered that an American girl had been murdered by a
graduate student and that, not only had he killed her, but
he had chopped her up into pieces and thrown her body
into the river in black plastic rubbish sacks. I had not been
in Cambridge long – I'd done my teacher training in
London, and the school I'm at now had been my first job.
They lowered the water level in the Cam, exposing the
muddy skeletons of bicycles and shopping trolleys. The
whole town could talk of nothing else.

There were plenty of notable murders in England,

even then. Plenty of young women who went missing – estate agents, secretaries, teenagers. But at the time this news story was especially gripping; it was gruesome, it was local, Bill was my own age. For a while my friends and I looked at our boyfriends with new eyes, as if they too might be capable of such a thing.

At the end of his letter, Bill said he would understand if I wanted to end our friendship, now that I knew what he had done. I got out of bed, and read the letter again. I read his confession over and over. *I killed my American girlfriend Iris because I was jealous of her, and she no longer loved me.* At first I felt angry, enraged, at what he had done. He had murdered a girl, a young woman, who had once been as alive as me. I had been tricked into liking him, into getting close. And I was angry that he hadn't told me the full story, that he hadn't added the words *and then I chopped up her body*. I stayed for a long while curled up on my sofa, staring at the letter and the late-night telly.

By morning I knew that he couldn't have written those final words to me. And he would never be able to say them to me either. How could you ever admit something like that? How could you ever tell someone you cared for, someone you hoped would be your friend? I wondered if perhaps Bill knew that I would remember. He knew that I was already living in Cambridge at the time of Iris's death. Maybe this was his way of telling me, *Laura*, he was saying, *and then I chopped her up*. Why does the fact that he dismembered her body make it any worse a crime? Iris was already dead, after all. He could have done anything to her, nothing could have been worse than what he had done already. And getting rid of the body did have a kind of logic to it, he had gone so far beyond anyway.

And that was the point when I could have ended it, I could have let the American girl and her death live for me, I could have pushed Bill away. But I didn't. Something in me empathized with Bill, something in me wanted to absolve him, redeem him, forgive. Perhaps this is what I have in common with all those female fans of Ted Bundy.

After two days I sat down and wrote Bill a letter. I said I appreciated his honesty. I said I wasn't there to sit in judgement, he had already been judged and found guilty. I said I was glad to be his friend, his companion.

From then on, our relationship was changed. The next time I went for a visit, Bill came into the room and we embraced. He was bigger than me, a lot taller, but I could feel his body trembling. He sat down at the table, and his eyes were watery. That day we could hardly speak.

I began to visit once every month. The intimacy of our letters increased.

I had been seeing a man for about six months, another teacher at my school. David was seven years younger than me, and very good-looking, and we'd been sleeping together most weekends. I had told Bill about him from the beginning, there was no reason not to, and I thought it might help ease the natural tension between us, between men and women over this kind of thing. But I began to find that when I was with David I was thinking about Bill. I decided to end it one Friday night; we'd been to a party and were both a little drunk. When I came out of the bathroom David had taken off all his clothes and was displaying himself for me. The first thought that came into my mind was that I wished he was Bill.

I wrote and told Bill I had stopped seeing David. Two days later I received a reply. It began like this:

Dear Laura,

I can't stop thinking about you.

If I was a free man, and you and I were together, this is what I would do. I would lift your dress over your head. I would take down your tights. I would unfasten your bra, and I would push down your knickers. And I would look at you, I would look at your body, and then I would do whatever you asked. Anything at all, anything to give you pleasure. And you could do anything you wanted with me. I want to feel myself inside you, I want to take you while you are sleeping, I want to be with you always.

I had never heard such words from a man, I never had and never thought I might.

From there we took off, we really did, we wrote nearly every day, and I increased my visits to fortnightly, which was the maximum he was allowed. Those two hours on Saturday afternoon were extreme, febrile, and devastating. The visits room, with all its noise and smell and disappointment, would fade away and Bill and I would be together somewhere else, anywhere else. We'd talk and talk and hold hands and look into each other's eyes.

'How was your week?'

'Oh, it was fine. I didn't do much other than go to school, do my preparation.'

'You work too hard.'

'No, I don't. How about you? What did you do?'

He laughed. 'I went to the gym, I washed the floors on all the landings, I read two novels, and I waited.'

In a sense we were both waiting. We didn't paw each other like other couples, I didn't sit in his lap. It was an old-fashioned courtship, stately, restrained, bound by rules and codes. The prison guards were our chaperones and we did not try to evade them. We were proud, and we were waiting for each other, we were waiting for Bill's release.

I don't think I've ever waited for anything before. I grew up in a generation that is accustomed to sexual gratification, to getting it when you want it, with ease. And I do think that is the way it should be. But with Bill it was different, of necessity. I had never been so continuously and completely excited. On Saturdays when I left the prison I would have to pull over to the side of the road and take deep breaths to still my heart, to quieten my body. In bed on my own at night I dreamt of sex and fucking and Bill.

I don't know why I liked him so much, indeed, why I had come to love him. But can we ever say why it is we love someone? I liked the way he looked, I liked the way he talked, I liked the way he carried himself. He had a very happy laugh, and when he laughed I felt I could see right inside him, into his heart which was open and warm. I liked the way that he liked me.

I'll admit it, there is something odd about falling in love with a prisoner. A captive man, a man in chains, a man rendered powerless. I felt he needed me, and I found that seductive. But not the fact that he was a murderer, not the fact that he had taken the life of a young American. Once I got to know him I discovered that he still had, or rather, what he had done still had a certain amount of notoriety in Cambridge. Every once in a while someone would mention the student who had been murdered. After I got to know Bill it happened once at school, and I kept myself from flinching. But that wasn't part of what I wanted in Bill, that was not part of it for me.

There were some weeks when I couldn't visit because Bill was seeing his parents. They lived in Leicester and were retired, his sisters both lived nearby. He said his sister Liz had wept throughout every one of their visits over the past decade. The other, Susan, had never been to visit him. One day, out of the blue, I received a phone call from Mrs Porter, Bill's mum.

'We would like to invite you to come to Leicester for lunch next week,' she said very quickly, her words almost, but not quite, stumbling. 'Bill has told us all about you, and we would very much like to meet you.' I began to speak, but she wouldn't let me. 'My husband and I could drive down to Cambridge and fetch you, it's quite quick these days, it wouldn't be any trouble, none at all.' She seemed to run out of words.

'That would be very nice,' I said, more out of shock than anything else, 'I can drive up myself.'

'Are you sure?'

'Yes.'

'Sunday week? About one o'clock?'

'Don't go to too much bother – '

'It will just be something light.'

She gave me directions, and we said goodbye.

Bill and I had decided against using the telephone to communicate with each other. Phone cards were expensive for him and the telephone on his wing afforded little privacy. I wasn't allowed to ring in. But at that point I wished I could pick up the phone, that I could call him and we could have a laugh and make this meeting with his parents a little less odd, a little less out of the ordinary.

That week in school was very busy. One of my favourite students was having difficulty. His parents had broken up, and it was as though when they divided their possessions, they had split him as well. He had been caught pissing against a wall in the gymnasium. Teaching was always hectic and stressful, but events like these added to the strain. When Friday came I felt exhausted. Bill and I had no visit that week, and Saturday was empty. By Sunday morning I was wound tight.

I drove up to Leicester and found their house rather too easily. I sat in the car for a while, until I began to feel conspicuous on the suburban street, among the gardeners, lawn-mowers, and dog-walkers. I went up the footpath, knocked on the door, and held my breath.

Mrs Porter answered. She gave me a big hug, unable to speak. Mr Porter stood behind her. He wore a cardigan, she wore an apron. You would not have believed their son was a murderer. They were both effusive in their welcoming. We went into the sitting room where I was introduced to Liz. She was tall like Bill and I could see she was someone I could easily have known, someone who was just like me. We sat down – Mrs Porter offered tea, Mr Porter insisted on sherry. 'Put the drive behind yourself,' he said, 'be at ease.'

They were very anxious to know me. 'Bill hasn't had a friend for a long time,' said Mrs Porter, placing special emphasis on the word 'friend'. 'He's such a loving person,' she said, and then she blushed, realizing she might have gone too far, given that we'd just met. His crime filled the air between us. I pushed forward, nodding and smiling. I felt as though we didn't need to speak, that words were awkward, there was such a lot we shared anyway. Liz alternated between being playful and funny, and on the edge of tears – the brother she knew on the one hand, the brother she couldn't know on the other. When we sat down to lunch it was a little uncomfortable. There were empty chairs, and at first I thought they had laid a place for absent Bill. Mr Porter noticed me looking.

'Susan and Jeremy,' he explained.

'They said they'd come,' Mrs Porter said, more to him than me.

'I know love,' he said. 'But I didn't think they would.'

'They said they'd come,' said Mrs Porter.

Liz changed the subject.

Lunch was not light, but proper and elaborate, right down to the trifle and the cheese. Mr Porter – he insisted I call him William, and his wife, Elizabeth, and I found the doubling of names reassuring – was pouring the coffee, when the front door opened and Susan arrived.

She marched up to the table angrily. Liz was like Bill, but Susan was like them both, that strange and beguiling blending of features that you sometimes see between siblings.

'Why did you invite her?' she demanded of her mother, not looking at me. 'Why are you having her in this house?'

'Susan, calm down, she – '

'Don't tell me to calm down. I am calm. We don't want anything to do with her – with him.'

Liz stood and went towards her sister. 'Susan – '

'He's not our brother any more,' she said, her voice hard and brittle.

'Susan,' Liz said, low, hypnotic, 'Susan.' She took her sister by the shoulders and turned her away from the table. She began to speak in a tone so quiet none of us could hear. They walked towards the front door.

'She'll take her out to the car,' said Elizabeth, reassuringly, as though this happened all the time.

193

'They'll go out to her car,' William added.

We drank our coffee in the sitting room. At lunch we had begun to talk about Bill, about his childhood, subjects we found fascinating. I could have listened to them all day. As I went to sit down I glanced out the window and saw Liz and Susan seated in the car. Susan was slumped on the steering wheel, and Liz was leaning over, stroking her hair. They looked comfortable somehow, and I wanted to be out there with them, on the back seat, listening.

And then things began to happen. Bill was supposed to start having home leave. He kept getting it set up, they'd agree to one day in Cambridge, I organized with the Porters that we would converge at my place, and then the leave would fall through. Cutbacks on prison staff, continual changes in policy. Bill wrote letter after letter of complaint to the officials. He said he thought the prison's incompetence might help him with his probation application. He had a hearing coming up in June. He had been in prison for twelve and a half years at that time. We worked hard to keep our expectations in perspective; his tariff, recommended by the judge at the time of sentencing, was ten years, so we thought it likely that he would have to serve at least thirteen. He went up before the board on Wednesday, we had arranged that he would ring me at school at lunch time. That morning I paced back and forth in the classroom and let the students do as they pleased. I had expected them to riot, but they seemed intimidated by me suddenly, and they remained in their seats meekly. At lunch I rushed to the staffroom and stood by the phone, scaring off anyone who tried to use it. I hadn't told any of my colleagues about Bill, in fact, I hadn't told any of my friends, nor my parents. It's not the easiest thing to tell people, 'I've got a new boyfriend, he wears a ball and chain.'

The phone rang, I picked it up and almost dropped it. 'Bill?' I said.

There was no reply. I could hear the prison echoing in the background, the sound of doors, men, and keys.

'Bill?' I said. I heard him draw a sharp breath. He was crying. I knew that he had not succeeded. It would be another year until his next parole board hearing.

That year passed amazingly quickly. I spent Christmas with my parents in Brighton, then drove up to Leicester on Boxing Day. Susan and Jeremy were there, as well as Liz, and even Susan was more at ease with me. The next time I went to the prison for a visit, I overheard one woman speaking to another in the queue to get inside. 'I went up to his parents on Boxing Day,' she said, 'it were right nice, they were right good to me.' She was small and pudgy and had dyed blonde hair; she was wearing a distressed denim mini-skirt, a white bomber jacket, bare legs, and cheap, dirty shoes with high heels. I saw with a shock that she was a convict's girlfriend, just like me; we were both convicts' girlfriends queuing up on visits day.

It was a dreamy time, that time before Bill was released. It was like one long extended Valentine's Day. I wrote love letters, I received love letters. We consummated our passion over and over again on the page. If someone else read our letters – and I often wondered if the screws did read them, they still practised a kind of censorship security – they would have found a strange mixture of trivia, romance, and pornography. *I want to feel myself inside you, I want to take you while you are sleeping, I want to be with you always.* We prompted great flights of fantasy in each other. I'd never known anything like it before.

And then it happened. When we least expected it. Another parole board hearing. Bill had been tipped off by his probation officer beforehand — it wouldn't happen. No explanation, it just wasn't his turn. We made the same arrangement nonetheless — he would telephone at lunch time. I worried all morning, but I was able to work. However, in the staffroom I guarded the phone.

It rang. I picked it up.

'Laura,' he said, 'Laura, you're not going to believe this, but they've given me my licence.'

I didn't reply.

'Laura,' he said, 'will you come and get me?'

3

AFTER EIGHT

Laura's little house near the Cam was two up, two down, big enough for her and her boyfriend. Bill was unused to having so much space. She gave him his own room, next to hers, although they intended to spend every night in her bed. In fact his room was bed-less, having only a little brown settee. But the room also had a door, and a desk, and in this it resembled his cell, and Bill found it a useful retreat.

When he was first released it was summer, long, bright hot days, and soon Laura's school broke up for the holidays. They spent their time cycling in the country-side, going for long walks, afternoons by the outdoor lido on Jesus Green. Laura told people she was going away, and they didn't see anyone but each other.

She drove out to the prison to pick him up and it was just like in a movie. She waited outside the prison gate. After a long while, the gate opened, and there he was, alone, clutching an old suitcase. He took one tentative step, testing the water, and another, and another, and when no one stopped him, he rushed forward and into Laura's arms. They got into her car and pulled out of the car park, and his head was spinning. The trees were too green, the sky too blue, it was as if he'd been blindfolded for thirteen and a half years and once again could see. He was afraid to look at the prison in case someone was there, waiting to drag him back, bang him up in solitary.

He looked at Laura as he held her. 'Hello,' he said, 'hello Laura.' And he began to laugh, his throat open wide, shouting with laughter, gulping the air with joy and fear and the rushing years of longing. He wound down the window of the car and leaned his head out, hoping to slough it off, blow it out, the dirt of the prison, the stain of the years he had spent locked away.

And Laura laughed too, she laughed with him, although for one moment as she looked at him – his hands on his thighs, his new jeans and shirt his mother had sent – she felt a little afraid. Did she know him? Who was he? But he turned to her smiling a smile greater than any she had ever seen, and he surged into her heart and she remembered everything that she loved about him.

His parents and sisters were waiting at her house, waiting for Laura to bring him home. 'They're very excited,' Laura said, 'they are dressed up, as if they're going to a wedding,' and she blushed when she heard what she had said.

'I can hardly wait,' he said, 'I can hardly wait to get there.' And he turned towards her again, he couldn't wait any longer, he had to touch her right away.

She pulled the car off the road, down a private lane. Through the trees they could see a large house. They walked into the woods, away from the house, sure they would find an open meadow of flowers, or a silky patch of grass. But there was only more woods, and brambles, and broken-down fences. Laura stopped and leaned against a tree. Her heart pounded low in her stomach.

'Come here,' she said.

Bill was looking up at an oak, the thick pavilion of leaves. He walked towards her, and soon he leaned into her. He felt large and strong and she could smell the prison lingering beneath his scent. They held each other very tight, squeezing themselves together. Bill thought Laura felt small and strong; she smelled of lemons and perfume. Laura thought they would make love right there, against the tree, but they did not. Bill said he wanted to wait, he wanted to wait until they were alone, in her house, in her bed, in the night. They had waited a long time and a few more hours would only increase their pleasure, not lessen it.

So that first day was a day of love, and upset, and exclamations. Susan and Jeremy were at Laura's house with William and Elizabeth and Liz, and it was the first time Bill had seen his eldest sister since his arrest. He had missed her wedding. When Laura opened the door of her house, there was a thick silence and for a moment she thought they had gone away, they had changed their minds and abandoned the reunion. But then they burst forward, Liz with her usual tears, William and Elizabeth grinning hugely. While they were waiting they had prepared lunch, but in their joy this was forgotten, and the turkey began to smoulder as they raised a glass of wine, Bill's first red wine in thirteen and a half years, and he thought it tasted rich and slow and thick. Elizabeth smelt the bird first and ran into the kitchen.

Bill felt as though he himself might burst into flame, as though all his nerve-endings were on fire. The wine went straight to his head and he turned to Laura and said, 'You mustn't give me any more. I'm like a child who has never had a drink.'

'Have you really not had a drink in all this time, Bill?' Liz asked as if she couldn't fathom such a thing.

'Prison hooch doesn't count,' said Bill, 'it just doesn't count. In prison I sometimes drank because I wanted to drown.' He paused, still smiling and relaxed, while the others teetered, their faces about to collapse, as if they didn't want to be reminded, as if they had thought that now he was released it would be as though it had never happened. He had never gone away, he had never been in prison, he had never murdered Iris.

'That's right,' said William, saving the day, 'we've got to watch out for our new boy. He's been away.' And the family sat down to dinner in Laura's house and toasted Bill and toasted each other and celebrated every Christmas and every birthday they had missed.

Susan was not flushed and giggling like her mother and her sister, she did not have a lot to say. Every now and then Bill looked at her, tried to engage her, but she was giving nothing away. Halfway through the meal, she got up and went into the kitchen to get another bottle of wine. Bill followed her and the others tried not to notice, they upped the volume of their conversation.

'Susan,' Bill said. It was a day of carefully enunciated names. 'Susan, it doesn't matter, you know.'

She would not look at him, she remained stooped in front of the fridge.

'It doesn't matter, I don't care that you never came to visit – I mean I care, but it is all right. I understand. There is no reason for you to forgive me. And you don't have to see me now that I've been released.'

Susan turned. She did not want to see him, it was true. She had hoped he would never be released, she would have been happy if he had disappeared completely. If he asked she would have told him he had ruined her life. Standing there, Bill could see how Susan felt, and something in him was prepared for that.

'I'm here for Mum and Dad,' she said.

Bill drew a breath. 'Okay,' he said, 'that's fine.' He took a step forward, Susan took a step further away. Bill dropped his hands to his sides. 'It's really good to see you. You look exactly the same.' He turned and went back into the other room. Susan leaned against the counter and pressed the cool bottle of wine against her face.

The hours passed and Bill's father William drank too much, got a little maudlin, kissed his wife, and fell asleep. Liz was driving her parents home, Bill helped them out to the car. Susan and Jeremy had left earlier. The summer night was warm and still, and yet they had remained indoors instead of sitting in Laura's garden. They wanted to keep that afternoon completely private, they wanted to shut themselves away.

And then Bill closed the door and the house felt empty and he and Laura were alone there for the first time. She thought him very handsome as he came to her, and he thought her a great beauty. Music was playing in the sitting room and they danced a little in the lamp-light, their feet moving smoothly over the carpet. Bill felt as though his brain was malfunctioning a little, flickering back and forth between the thirty-seven years he was aged now, and the twenty-four-year-old he had been last he was free. Laura couldn't get close enough to him as they danced, she couldn't believe he was here, now, and to stay. After a long while they kissed. And then they went upstairs to Laura's bed. What happened there was remarkable and profound; they thought that together they were truer and better than their individual selves had ever been. *I want to feel myself inside you, I want to take you while you are sleeping, I want to be with you always.*

Summer ended and Laura went back to work. She and Bill had developed a strategy – she would say they had met on holiday, it was a whirlwind romance, he had moved in as soon as he could, he'd been a student at Cambridge but had been away. In Canada. He'd been working in Canada, in oil exploration up north. If anyone asked, that would be what she would tell them. And they did ask, of course they asked, first day back, and Laura blushed as she told her lies. Her colleagues assumed she blushed with embarrassment and passion and, of course, that was true as well.

The terms of Bill's licence – he had explained to Laura that a life sentence is indeed life; the state keeps track of lifers once they are released and he would be on probation for the rest of his days – were such that he could do pretty much as he pleased, apart from break the law and leave the country. The stated terms – he kept the sheaf of papers in his desk in the room Laura had given him — included a clause that demanded he 'disclose' his crime to any woman with whom he became involved. Probation officers and the police would pay special attention to any relationship he formed. If they had any reason to suspect he was repeating a pattern, that he was in any way replicating his relationship with Iris, they could take him in, whisk him off the street and back into prison, no need for a trial or hearing. But as far as Bill's probation officer was concerned, this was not an issue. Laura knew about Bill's crime, Laura was not an eighteen-year-old girl, Laura and Bill would be all right. The probation officer had a large, unwieldy case-load, most of the ex-cons with whom he worked were a lot worse off than Bill.

Bill knew it would be difficult to find a job; he'd have to disclose his record to any potential employer. And who would want to hire a murderer with a doctorate, for a dishwasher, for a lectureship? He received a tiny income from the state by claiming he was Laura's lodger, and his parents gave him the money they had saved expressly. He and Laura had discussed it thoroughly, he would not have to get work right away. He could take his time, find his civilian feet, figure out the best way to live. He went running, did the shopping, cleaned the house, and cooked Laura dinner.

Laura had never thought it odd that Bill was willing to come back to Cambridge. She was in Cambridge, he'd been in Cambridge, it was a good place to be. Part of her — most of her — was happy to live as though the thing, the horrible thing, had never happened. Iris. They did not talk about it, about her. That was simply the way it felt best, that made it possible to live.

'What did you do today, sweetheart?' she said as she dropped her books on the table one day after school.

Bill was wearing an apron, holding a wooden spoon. 'I went to the city library. I wandered around the town a bit. I went to my old college.'

'You did?'

'I ran into one of my tutors.'

Laura asked a normal question, sometimes she did it just to see what it was like. 'Did he remember you?'

Bill laughed. 'Yes. It took him a few moments to place me, but when he did . . . He tried hard not to be terrified.'

Laura gasped and then smiled.

'That will give them something to talk about at High Table. He told me that Dr Simms died.'

'Dr Simms?'

'My old supervisor. The one who used to sleep through supervisions. In fact, he died during a supervision. His students didn't even realize it. They tiptoed out of the room like usual. It was left to the bedder to find him the next day.'

Laura lifted the lid off the pot Bill was simmering.

'I feel bad about him, Dr Simms,' he said. 'I sort of admired the old guy.'

It was October now and although the days were often sunny, the warmth did not linger in the evening. Laura closed the door to the garden. Bill followed her into the sitting room. She drew the curtains and sat down on the sofa. Bill sat next to her, drawn to her in a way that had become nearly familiar. They folded themselves into each other's arms and slipped off each other's clothes one piece at a time. Bill could not get over the revelation of Laura's body, the way she gave it him, the way she let him touch her as he desired. He stroked her stomach, soft and slightly rounded, and further down, he moved his fingers through her pubic hair. He held her shoulders as he penetrated her, and, later, as he moved in her, he gripped her waist and kissed her neck. They took up a rhythm from which he could not and did not want to escape.

Laura had never felt about anyone the way she felt about Bill. When they fucked she moved beyond herself, into him, with him. For him it was as though every day was a kind of unexpected bonus, and Laura was amazed to find herself included in that. Bill gave her rapture. It didn't matter that he couldn't work, that he was, essentially, her dependent, that her social life had disappeared and her friends thought her a stranger. Laura was happy, she had never been so happy, and it was even more complete when Bill was inside her, in her house, in her arms. She cried out when she came, and he laughed and held her.

Christmas approached and they planned to spend Christmas Eve in Brighton with Laura's parents, travelling up to Leicester on Christmas Day. They drove down to the coast and Laura felt a little nervous; her parents had not met Bill. Over the phone she had told them the same story she told everyone else. Laura hadn't lived with a man in years and it had been a long time since she'd brought anyone to meet her mother and father.

The first hours in Brighton passed stiffly. Laura's parents were not like Bill's, they did not open their front door and step into an embrace. They conducted themselves with Bill as though they were interviewing a prospective employee. Laura's father was a retired headmaster, her mother had never worked, and they led a country life of bridge games and fêtes for charity. Her mother had laid out towels for them both – in separate bedrooms. After dinner Bill sat in front of the television, while Laura rounded on her parents in the kitchen.

'I'm thirty-seven years old, Mother! I can sleep with whomever I choose.'

'Don't speak to your mother that way,' warned her father, always his first contribution to any argument.

'How can you invite us here and then treat us like naughty children?'

'I don't know who invited *him*,' her mother said, her voice very tight, 'but it wasn't me.'

'Who is he?' her father demanded.

'What do you mean?' asked Laura.

'Well, who is he? He seems to have appeared from nowhere. What has he been doing for the past fifteen years? I asked him about Canada – about the oil – but he was . . . well, he was terribly vague. He doesn't know a thing about oil exploration, Laura, does he?'

'Have you been lying to us, Laura?' her mother asked.

She attempted to back-track. 'It's all right about the rooms – it's only one night. It won't happen again.' She went towards the door.

'Don't you turn your back on us, Laura! We want to know who he is. What are you hiding from us?'

Laura turned and looked at her mother. She felt tired, perhaps it might be easier to tell them, to get it out in the open, to end the pretence. It was Christmas, after all, maybe they'd be full of Christian charity.

'Has he been in gaol?' asked her father.

Laura gasped. 'How did you know?'

'Oh, it's written all over him,' her father said. 'From the way he rolls his cigarettes to the way he eats . . .'

'The way he eats?' Laura objected.

'. . . as though any moment someone is going to snatch away his plate – to the way he looks at you.' Her father grimaced.

'Why didn't you tell us?' asked her mother.

'I didn't think you'd approve.'

'We don't,' they said simultaneously. Then they all turned to look; Bill was standing in the door. Laura's father took a deep breath. 'You are not welcome here,' he said, his words directed at Bill.

'All right,' said Laura, 'we'll leave.'

Not working was more difficult than Bill expected; in prison he had always had a job, even if it was slopping out shit for an hour a day. He was already heavily overqualified, and he didn't want to continue to study. In the autumn he had tried to get a job in the local sandwich bar, but when he disclosed, as he had to, they sent him away, horrified. He no longer went there for sandwiches. His probation officer offered to get him on a government training scheme, but it sounded like make-work to him, and he didn't want to be involved with other ex-cons. He thought about volunteer work, but by then he was gripped by a kind of sloth. He was accustomed to long hours of doing nothing, so he wasn't bored, and he didn't mind not having money. But he was growing restless.

And then it was January and very dark and the sky touched the ground without lifting. Bill told Laura Januarys were very difficult in prison and he was surprised to find that outside they were almost as bad. There were icy winds in Cambridge and he wore layer upon layer of clothes when he went out running. His body had changed a lot in the six months since his release, he had slimmed down, lost the beef he had built up through the gym and prison food. At Christmas he had retrieved his stuff from his parents' house, and found that he could still wear his old clothes. Sometimes when he ran he felt as though he were re-inhabiting his body, regaining something he had lost, catching up with it. He ran down paths familiar from his student days, past young men whom he imagined could be his former self. He began to deviate from his usual route of Laura's house to the river, across the commons, through the town.

One day he found himself outside his old house, the house he had shared with Geoff and Raj and Tim. The house where he had loved Iris. The house where she had died. He stood opposite, on the far side of the road, and he realized with a shock that there were parts of Cambridge he'd been avoiding. Nothing about the house had changed, it looked as though the same roof tiles were still missing. A young man came along the pavement and turned into the footpath, and Bill faced the other direction, to hide the fact that he was watching. The man unlocked the door and went in. For a moment, Bill was back inside that house, back inside the time when he had lived there with his friends, when he had known the American girl.

He stood in the dark. Lights went on and off in different rooms, on different floors, but no one else arrived, or left. Later, a car pulled up and the passenger door opened. Bill watched as a young woman climbed out. She was small, and she had long dark hair. She walked up the footpath. Bill crossed the road as the car pulled away. She was knocking on the door as Bill reached the gate. He raised his hand and said something, he didn't know what, and as the girl turned to look at him, the front door opened, and a harsh light fell on her face. Bill saw she wasn't Iris, and he backed into the darkness. He pulled up his hood and ran down the street.

January was difficult for Laura as well. Having a dependent, even one as accommodating as Bill, was hard to get used to, tougher than she had anticipated. Her teacher's wage went a lot less further for two and she found she was having to think carefully about simple things like going to the cinema, out to eat. She and Bill had spent six months hunkered down together, not wanting to see other people. This anti-social behaviour suited them both, and it meant they avoided having to explain about Bill's life, having to lie. But Laura was beginning to miss her friends. In recent times she and a group of teachers had gone skiing together during the winter-term break and when talk in the staffroom came round to this year's trip, Laura realized with a pang that she wouldn't be going. Bill wasn't allowed to leave the country yet and, besides, it was out of the question.

'Which resort?' she asked Elise one day.

'We're going to go to Courmayeur this year, Italy, it's cheaper than France.'

'Hotel or chalet?'

'We've got a whole chalet to ourselves, so that will be great.' Elise paused and poured extra sugar in her coffee. 'We didn't – I mean – we just assumed you wouldn't be going.'

'You did?'

'Yes, well, you and Bill seem so – well, I know how it is when you fall in love . . .' she sang the last few words and laughed. 'Maybe next year you can both come? Does Bill ski?'

'Yes,' said Laura, 'yes he does,' although she did not know whether or not he did.

The next week Elise asked Laura if she wanted to go out for a drink, as though she had seen a crack in Laura's armour and was determined to widen it. Laura agreed, she said yes, it would be just the two of them.

When she told Bill her plans, his face fell. She watched as he quickly reconciled himself to the news.

'I can't expect to have you to myself all the time, can I?' he said. 'We do live in the world, after all.'

'Yes,' said Laura, sadly, as though she was agreeing with much more than what he had just said.

So she began to go out with her friends from time to time, and soon irregular get-togethers became once a week. She did not ask Bill if he wanted to come, because, truth be told, she enjoyed getting away on her own. Bill had a certain level of engagement with the world, a particular intensity bred by years spent locked away. Eight in the evening until eight in the morning – these were rough hours for him, the hours during which he'd been banged up on his own every night. Some evenings Laura felt him slip away from her after eight, as though he could no longer occupy any realm other than his own. He might go upstairs to his little room where he had his desk and his door and his radio, or he might remain next to her in front of the television, but either way, he wasn't really there. It didn't happen every night but, even when he coped well, he would generally go to bed before her. She would crawl in several hours later, and he would wake up disoriented, a bit confused, and they would make love, and it would go well.

Laura felt terrible about her parents' reaction to Bill; she hadn't had any contact with them since. She had never got on well with them, but she didn't want to have to think about what might happen next, how she would ever patch things up with them. It was yet another area of her life that she would have to keep separate from Bill. She had hoped that Christmas with the Porters would cure any bitterness her lover might feel, and on the day he had seemed happy and whole and optimistic. Bill kept his shadow close by him, Laura had always known that, but now the shadow felt darker, colder, and closer as well.

One evening she and Elise were out on their own.

'Okay,' said Elise, 'you've got to tell me about Bill. Who is this guy and why are you two so reclusive – I can understand, when you first fall in love, but come on, we'd like to meet him. He's part of you.'

Laura looked at her friend's face, and thought her lovely and candid, without guile. Surely Elise would be sympathetic? 'Well,' she said, suddenly full of resolve, 'I'll tell you. Bill . . .' she paused.

'Yes?' said Elise. 'Come on.'

'Bill got out of prison last June.'

Elise stared at her without speaking.

'He was in for a long time. He – '

Elise interrupted. 'You met him through that scheme, didn't you? That volunteer thing you used to do – writing and visiting prisoners. I always thought that was strange.'

'Elise!'

'Well, you had your pick, Laura. Everybody wanted to go out with you. Even my ex-husband used to ask if you were seeing anyone.'

'George?'

'Yes, George, the dirty old fool.'

'There's nothing wrong with Bill, he just did something wrong, that's all.'

'What?'

Laura looked at Elise.

'What did he do?'

Oh fuck, thought Laura, here we go. 'He killed his girlfriend.'

'What?' Elise shrieked. In the pub heads turned.

'He was young, she was young . . . It was a long time ago.'

'Oh, and that makes it all right?'

'It doesn't make it all right, it's just that . . . he wasn't a criminal.'

'No, not a criminal, only a murderer — what on earth do you mean?'

'He didn't rob banks or deal drugs or anything — he'd never done anything wrong before.'

'Beginner's luck then?'

'Elise — '

'What do you expect me to say? "Oh, that's great Laura, your boyfriend's a cold-blooded killer, cool." No.' She shook her head. 'No, no, no.' She paused and looked at Laura for an explanation that Laura was not able to give. 'How do you know he won't do it again?'

'I know him, I trust him — '

'How do you know he won't do it to you, he won't kill you? Do you know that for sure, Laura? Could you give me a guarantee?'

Laura looked at her drink. It had been the right tactic, avoiding telling anybody about Bill. She wished she had stuck to it. 'I'm sorry I told you,' she said, and she felt an awful thing: ashamed of Bill and, then, ashamed of her shame. 'Don't tell anyone,' she said. 'Please.'

'Oh Laura, I only worry about you. Shit,' Elise rapped the table with her knuckles. 'Damn,' she said, shaking her head.

'I guess this means you won't be inviting us around for dinner,' Laura said.

Elise laughed a little and said, 'Fuck, I don't know.'

And during the evenings that Laura was out with her friends, Bill began to go out too. He started to go running after eight. He'd go up to his little room, close the door and pull on his layers of clothes, the noise of the prison echoing in his head. He'd got rid of everything else, the prison smell, the prison habit of hoarding matches and tobacco and library books, the prison touchiness, always keeping his back against the wall, but whatever he did, he could not get rid of the noise. Some nights it echoed in his brain like his head was a rattle, a gourd with a pebble trapped in it. Every time he moved, he heard it. He thought running might dislodge it, roll it away.

At night Cambridge was as dark as it had been when he was a student. The Backs were not lit, nor were the commons, but where he had feared it before, he loved it now, he parted the darkness and ran on through the black. It was as though he was hidden in the dark, the city was hiding him. He began to trace a new route. He'd head up to the college where Iris had been a student, to the residence where he had lain on her bed and waited for her to finish seeing her friends. He'd run down past the house where he used to live with Geoff and Raj and Tim. He'd run round the back of his old college and climb over the fence and run around the empty garden shed. They'd moved the tools elsewhere, he wondered if that was because of him, because of what he had done, and he hoped he hadn't caused too much trouble. Then he ran down to the river, to the bank where he had dropped the black plastic rubbish sacks with Iris in them. But once he reached the river, he was unable to keep running. He stopped suddenly, dizzy with lack of air. He staggered along for a few paces, trying to get his breath back, his legs to move. He stopped and fell to his knees. Occasionally in the cold night he had witnesses, usually he did not, it didn't matter. Once someone came to his aid, but he shouted at them, 'Fuck off, fuck off,' and they did. He would lie down across the path like a drunk, facing the river. And he'd watch the water flow by. And he'd think of Iris, of the small dark mole on her left breast, of her hands, of her feet, of her face. Her eyes, her iris eyes, violet. There was no forgetting, there could be no forgetting, not in prison serving his time, not now that he had been released.

After her conversation with Elise about Bill, Laura came home to an empty house. It was the first time she had come home to find Bill gone. She called out his name, went upstairs and knocked on the door of his room. She opened it, he wasn't there. She stepped inside. She hadn't spent much time in this room since Bill had moved in. It had once been her study, now his books were mixed up with hers. She looked at the things he had pinned to the wall, postcards mostly, from Liz and William and Elizabeth on their holidays. She hadn't turned on the lamp and light from the corridor filtered in, casting long silhouettes. It smelt of him, the room, musty and cigarettes. She closed the door and went downstairs.

A little while later, after midnight, Bill came in. Laura called out to him from the sitting room. He didn't answer, went straight upstairs. She followed.

'Bill,' she said, 'Bill?'

He wasn't in the bathroom or the bedroom. The door to the study was closed. She knocked, repeating his name. 'Are you there, sweetheart?' She opened the door, it did not have a lock.

The room was dark, so she turned on the overhead light. Bill was curled up on the brown settee, facing inward, his hood pulled over his head. His clothes were caked with mud and she could smell the river rising off him. She moved near him and rested her hand on his shoulder. She felt him shrink away.

Laura went to bed. She knew that re-entering the world was fraught with difficulty for ex-prisoners, she knew that all manner of things could be thrown up for them, none of which would be easy to deal with. She had read a pamphlet that Bill's probation officer had recommended; it said that ex-prisoners might need to be left on their own to come to terms with the missing years of their life, the years during which everyone else has got on with things while they've been locked away. The Rip Van Winkle effect – you wake up one day many years later and everything is changed.

In the middle of the night she heard Bill stirring. He was taking a bath. A little while later, he came into the bedroom. He got into bed in a new way, he climbed under the duvet from the bottom end. She felt his lips on her feet, her ankles. He was kissing her calves, her knees, her thighs. It took a long time, and it was delicious, and when his head emerged from under the covers, she could tell he was smiling as he pushed inside her, and she threw back her head and opened her arms and was his, she was his, she was his.

But things did not get better, they got worse. Bill began to go out after eight p.m. on nights when Laura was staying in. The length of time he stayed out got longer and longer. Laura tried to resist asking him what he was doing, she did not want to put unnecessary pressure on him, but eventually, she gave in.

'I run,' he said, 'you know I like to go running.'

'But for hours and hours, no one runs for hours and hours.'

'I do,' he said.

She didn't ask about the mud he carried back on his clothes, she didn't try to continue the conversation.

February and then March, and still he went out, running and running. Laura began to spend more time away from the house, with Elise and her other friends. But she didn't tell anyone about what Bill was doing; she had no one to tell. They made love less often and, when they did, sometimes it was painful.

'Where do you go?' she asked one night.

'To the river.'

'Why?'

'It's where I belong,' he said, turning away.

Laura began to panic. Bill was becoming a stranger, he was sinking deeper into himself. They had stopped having their happy evenings, their lovely weekends where they cooked for each other, did things to the house. She arranged for them to go visit the Porters in Leicester; Bill agreed to go, but he was not enthusiastic.

They drove up on Friday evening. The family was there, William and Elizabeth, Liz and Susan, and they had a party. William mixed cocktails, he'd been taking a

215

bartending course, 'for no good reason,' he said to Laura, 'except to drink!' After a few Margaritas, Liz began to tease Susan about Jeremy who had been unable to come.

'What's he doing, playing darts at your local?' Laura could tell Liz intended to sound light-hearted, but her tone was sharp and piercing.

'He doesn't play darts any more,' Susan said uneasily.

'What – too challenging?'

Susan looked at her sister. It was clear she couldn't think of a reply.

'Oh come on Susie, you can do better than that.' Liz reached out to tussle her sister's hair, but Susan took hold of her wrist, and twisted her arm backwards. Liz winced and, with her free hand, whacked Susan across the back of the head.

'Girls!' shouted William. 'Stop it.' He paused, adding, 'You're both nearly forty!' but his daughters ignored him as they grappled on the couch. Bill got up and left the room, followed by his mother. Laura stood up, unsure of what to do. William had turned away and was peering out the window of the sitting room. 'Look at those roses,' he said, shaking his head. Laura went to his side, but it was dark, and she couldn't see what he meant. Susan howled in anger and pain, and William and Laura both turned as she shot out of the room and up the stairs. Liz stayed on the sofa, suddenly calm as a cat, nonchalantly examining her nails. William sighed and went over and sat down next to his daughter, picking up the remote control for the TV.

Laura hovered in the door of the kitchen. The back door was ajar, she wondered if Bill and his mother had gone out into the garden. She went towards it, and she heard Elizabeth's voice, speaking very softly.

'It's all right, son, it's all right,' she was saying. Laura stood by the sink and leaned over to try and see out the window. The light above the door illuminated the patio as though it was a stage. Elizabeth and Bill were sitting at the far end, overlooking the grass. Bill's head was in his mother's lap, Laura could hear that he was weeping. 'I killed her, I killed her, and then I chopped her up,' he said, 'I killed her and now she will never leave me.' Elizabeth stroked his hair easily, as though his words cost her nothing to absorb. 'I killed her, I killed her, and then I chopped her up, and now she will never leave me.'

Laura turned away and shoved her hands deep into the pockets of her jeans. He could say these things to his mother, but not to her. For the first time ever she wished to God that she had never met him, and then she hated herself for having that thought. More and more, every day, there were things she could not think about, speak of. Every morning she made a huge effort to push it all away. She pushed it away for Bill, she pushed it away for herself. She wished she could push it away completely.

They went back to Cambridge and communication shut down between them even further. They still had sex, they still fucked each other, they couldn't stop that entirely. Bill's time-clock turned upside-down, as the nights grew warmer and shorter he began to stay out later, sleeping during the day. He'd slip into the house before dawn and climb into bed. When Laura got up, she'd find a muddy track through the house leading to the bedroom, his trainers, his clothes, his underwear. She'd pick everything up and put it in the washing machine.

One morning Laura woke to find Bill had pulled the duvet off the bed. He was standing in the corner, staring at her body. She sat up and tried to cover herself with her hands.

'Don't do that,' he said, his voice gentle and sweet. 'I want to see you, I want to look at you.' He came forward, he was naked and muddy, his penis erect. He grabbed hold of her ankles and pulled her down the bed towards him. Then he lowered himself onto her, as though in slow-motion. 'I really want this,' he said, 'I really want you.' Laura tried to relax, she tried to embrace him, but his skin felt very cold, clammy. He began to fuck her, he was slow and loving and she moved with him, feeling herself warming up. But suddenly he began to come, and in the midst of that she heard him whisper. 'Iris,' he said. 'Iris. Iris.' The next minute he was asleep.

Laura struggled out from beneath him. She went into the bathroom, feeling numb and dazed. In the mirror she saw there was mud on her breasts, on her shoulders and, to her horror, one clear mud handprint on her face. Shaking, she ran hot water in the sink and washed hurriedly. Wrapped in her bathrobe, she walked quickly through the house, picking up his things. In the kitchen she found the backpack that he always carried when he ran. She emptied the contents onto the table. She found the letter she had written to Bill in prison, she found a bread knife, she found some string, and she found a thick roll of black plastic rubbish sacks. Her heart stopped as she handled these things.

Desperate not to wake him, she tiptoed upstairs, grabbed her clothes, and went outside and got into her car. She tried to figure out what to do. She couldn't go to Bill's probation officer – if the authorities found out about his behaviour they would be sure to revoke his licence immediately. He'd be back in prison the same day, no questions asked. Whom could she tell? Not Elise, Elise would march round to the house, pack Bill's bag herself and force him to leave. Elise would call the police. He needed to see someone, he needed to do something, Laura thought, he needed her more than ever, even though she was afraid.

She went to school and fumbled through the day.

Bill woke up in mid-afternoon. The first thing he thought was, I'm going crazy, I am losing my mind. But then that clarity dissipated and he felt paranoia well up in its place. Do the shopping, he thought, do the shopping, clean the house, make everything very very nice. And so that was what he did for the next couple of hours and when Laura got home he was hanging out the washing. She seemed shy, he wondered why she seemed so shy, and he offered to cook her dinner, told her to sit down and get caught up with her work. She obeyed him, she was obedient. And he cooked supper, he cooked a wonderful meal, steak and mashed potatoes and courgettes in garlic, he got it all exactly right. They sat down, he lit candles and opened a bottle of red wine, and they ate and they drank and it was lovely. Afterwards they watched the news on TV. And then it was eight o'clock. He looked at his watch, the watch she had given him, and the little hand was on eight.

So he went upstairs and got changed, pulling on his layers, and he picked up his rucksack before he went out, turning around to go back and kiss Laura. Kiss Laura. Laura, my girlfriend. And he ran up to Iris's college, to the college where the young girl he had known, so long ago, the young woman, the American he had killed, where she lived. 'Oh yeah,' he said out loud to no one, 'my American girlfriend, that's where she lived, my old girlfriend, the one I killed.' No matter how often, how many ways he got himself to admit to it, no matter how loudly or bluntly or with how much careful consideration, that's what it came down to: Iris, I took her life, I did.

After Bill went out Laura sat in front of the television and watched soap operas and sitcoms and a police show and a hospital drama. She watched the news again, and it was nearly midnight. Then she went upstairs and hauled on her trainers and she went outside, in the dark, to look for Bill.

Down at the river the water flows smoothly and in the black night it is hard to see that it moves. It looks solid, almost, still, although you can hear it lapping, hissing, as though the water speaks with a lisp. The things that live on it during the day are gone – the birds, the punts, the tourists. It is impossible to tell what lies beneath the surface, how deep it is, what swims in its depths. Bill lay on the footpath and crept forward over the edge of the concrete embankment. He placed his hand lightly on the water, but even his hand was too heavy; it broke the tension and plunged through. It felt reedy, the water felt reedy between his fingers, even here where he knew it was not. He put his hands in the mud and pulled his body further out from the embankment, so that his face hung over the water. He looked down, it was too dark to see his reflection but he knew that it was there. He lowered his face into the water, very slowly. He broke the surface first with his forehead, then with his nose, then he pushed his whole face in and he thought it felt like penetrating a woman, Iris, Laura. He moved his head from side to side, feeling the pressure from upstream, the downstream flowing away. He let his body relax, and he felt like an otter as he slipped in.

Laura was out of breath as she ran along the river, heading upstream against the current. The moon was quite full, and gave the night a silvery light. She climbed up onto the footbridge and paused there, searching for Bill along the embankment. She looked down at the water and saw a dark shape float by. She ran to the bank, grabbed a stick, and fished the thing out of the water. It was a black rubbish bag. Empty, flat, and when she retrieved it, dripping. She dropped the stick and hurried along the water's edge. She came to a place opposite a low group of willow trees that swept the water like languid women. From beneath the branches, she watched as Bill's little rucksack emerged and floated away.

She tore off her jacket and leapt into the river in a tangle of her own arms and legs. She went deep under, and came up gagging, struggling as though she had never learned how to swim. Laura thrashed her way across the river, now fighting the current for real. She grabbed hold of the willow, and the tree parted its branches to let her in to where it held Bill. His body lay beneath the surface of the water as if, even in death, he was too heavy to float. Laura seized his shoulders and turned him over and cradled him in her arms. His eyes were closed and she saw once again how fine and dark his long lashes were. His lips looked stung, stung by her kisses, and she wanted to tell him she loved him and would love him always. The water flowed around them and his head moved slowly, it fell against her shoulder as though he was in a deep and captive sleep.